Karolinum Press

ABOUT THE AUTHOR

Siegfried (Salomon) Kapper (1821–1879) was a Czech-Jewish writer, scholar, and folklorist. He earned his medical degree in Vienna in 1847 and took part in the revolutionary movements of 1848 in that city, being elected to the Austrian parliament. That year he published a collection of poetry (*Befreite Lieder*), giving voice to that revolutionary spirit. While a student, he advocated strongly for Jewish emancipation and was sympathetic to Czech national aspirations. He notably published poetry in Czech (*České Listy*) as well as German, and he translated Bohemian and Moravian folksongs into German.

Kapper traveled through Central and Eastern Europe, developing an interest in the local cultures. He practiced medicine in several Bohemian towns before settling in Prague in 1867. There he became a civic and cultural figure, serving on various committees and giving lectures on literature and on Slavic culture. He translated collections of Serbian and other Balkan folklore, and penned popular travelogs of his journeys through Southeastern Europe.

Kapper's interest in Jewish matters never waned. The stories he wrote about the Jews of Prague (collected posthumously as *Prager Ghettosagen*) display both his intimate connection to Jewish themes and his intense interest in folkloristics. As a testament to the significance of his impact on Czech Jewish life, in 1920 the prominent association of Czech Jewish academics—Spolek Českých Akademiků Židů (Society of Czech Academic Jews)—changed its name to Akademický Spolek Kapper (Kapper Academic Society), and a year later published a collection of his writings.

Kapper died of tuberculosis in Pisa in 1879.

MODERN CZECH CLASSICS

Siegfried Kapper Tales of the Prague Ghetto

Translated from the German by Jordan Finkin

Afterword by Jindřich Toman

KAROLINUM PRESS 2022

KAROLINUM PRESS
Karolinum Press is a publishing department
of Charles University
Ovocný trh 560/5, 116 36 Prague 1
Czech Republic
www.karolinum.cz

Translated from Siegfried Kapper, *Prager Ghettosagen*, Prag:
Jakob B. Brandeis, 1896 (Jüdische Universal-Bibliothek, 38)
Cover and graphic design by Zdeněk Ziegler
Cover illustration from the book *Der alte Prager Judenfriedhof*
by L. Jeřábek, Prague 1903
Set and printed in the Czech Republic by Karolinum Press
First English edition

Cataloging-in Publication Data is available
from the National Library of the Czech Republic

ISBN 978-80-246-4945-0 (pbk)
ISBN 978-80-246-4946-7 (pdf)
ISBN 978-80-246-4947-4 (epub)
ISBN 978-80-246-4948-1 (mobi)

The moon emerged from the thick clouds right above Braník's monstrous limestone outcrops, scattering its magical light in a thousand glittering stars over the gently flowing waves of the Moldau. A profound silence lay over the waters and the surrounding landscape, broken only by the monotonous, rhythmic stroking of oars.

A skiff had set off from the shore by Braník and was gliding slowly and peacefully down the wide river.

The boy at the oars sang a pious hymn in long-held notes. Zerah stared at the floor of the skiff in front of him, lost in thought, as Golda leaned against the side of the little craft. She gazed down into the dark, mysterious depths as she toyed with a willow twig in the waves as if trying to fish those fleeting, glimmering little stars out of the water—stars which seemed to emerge from the deep to dance their moonlit roundelay on the softly rippling waves.

"My child, I promised to tell you the story of Genenda!" old Zerah broke the silence. "Would you like to hear it?"

"Yes! do tell it, Grandfather," Golda replied, pulling the willow twig out of the water and turning to face her grandfather.

"Come then, my child," he continued, urging the girl closer to him. "Come, sit on the bottom of the boat, over here, by me. It's not safe to sit near the edge, you might get dizzy. Good. Now I can start!"

Golda sat down on the floor of the boat, beside her grandfather, and lay her black locks on his knee, watching him with her large, dark eyes and listening attentively with expectant anticipation.

Zerah began: In the year 1040, the banks of this river were still hemmed with reeds from time immemorial, and dark, ancient forests stretched off over mountains and plains on either side. There was still little arable land and few fertile pastures, and there were neither villages nor farms to be seen scattered through the valleys to the right and left as they are today. Yet even then the proud Vyšehrad[1] loomed over those sharp rocks. Now you can only see the decaying walls and half-crumbled towers where princes once sat with their advisors deliberating over the welfare of the people, passing judgment on what was right and what was wrong. Even then our forefathers dwelt here in this land, with their houses and communities, and made their living honestly by the fruits of their labor according to the laws of the Book. They were still few in number and they did not yet live all together in their own quarter of the city, segregated from the other faith, separated by walls and gates. In the shelter of the prince's castle, at the foot of the Vyšehrad stood their few houses made of unbaked bricks and roofed with straw, relying on one another in pious community, pleasing to God.

In one of these houses, closer to the shore than the rest, lived Rabbi Baruch, known as the Chazan, or Cantor.[2] God had blessed him above so many others with the gift of song, and his understanding of string music exceeded anyone else at that time. Both became a rich source of profit for him. The whole week long he would wander the country with his songsters and his fiddle, enlivening the festivities of the noblemen in their castles and the burghers in their marketplaces. They paid him handsomely, for wherever he went good cheer followed, and wherever he brandished his bow hearts did not fail to rejoice.

However, on Friday evenings and on the Sabbath and holidays he stood before the Holy Ark, his singers at his side. He prayed with them out of a large Siddur,[3] singing Psalms, chanting the weekly Torah portion, and leading the congregation in their prayers. When the service came to an end, he returned with his singers to his house by the shore to spend his Sabbath rest in quiet domesticity, to pray from God's word, to nourish his soul and strengthen it for the week's worldly pursuits.

In the doorway Genenda would be waiting for him, the last of his darling children; the others, two sons and two daughters, had all been laid to rest a year ago. And shortly thereafter he had gone to bury their mother as well. Genenda was the only one left to him. She went out to meet him and greeted him with all her childlike sweetness, "Good Sabbath!" He kissed her, lay his hands on her head, and recited the blessing of the four Matriarchs over her. He then went inside where the table was spread with wine and cakes, all prepared for him and his singers. On the reading stand in the window nook his Talmud lay open so he could continue reading without having to leaf through to find the place he had stopped the previous Sabbath. All this Genenda had done to please her father. She would spend the whole day with him; for him she was the soul of the Sabbath.

He was content and lived happily like few other Jews. For he had achieved what a man requires to be happy: a sufficient living and a person who loves him and who deserves to be loved, his child.

One Sabbath—the Sabbath before Purim—shortly before the time for Minchah,[4] a stranger opened the door of his house.

Rabbi Baruch rose respectfully from his chair as the young man had very refined features, an elegant bearing, and looked much like the young nobility of the country. Rabbi Baruch noticed, however, that before entering the house this stranger touched the mezuzah,[5] his lips moving faintly as if he were praying. He then approached the Rabbi cheerfully. Rabbi Baruch recognized a son of Israel and extended his hand in welcome, "Is it well with you?"

The stranger answered, "Very well!"

Rabbi Baruch bade him come closer. "Who are you? Where have you come from? And what do you want in the house of Rabbi Baruch the Cantor? If you are in a hurry to tell me something important then do so at once. But if you are not pressed for time and your mission can wait, please be my guest at the third Sabbath meal, which I was just about to begin. Then you can speak with me of what you will."

"You are the master of the house!" the stranger replied. "Your wish is my own!"

Genenda had been reverently reading a book of Psalms. She had not even looked up when the stranger entered, for she was pious and God-fearing and it was a sin to interrupt one's reading of the Holy Book or one's prayers. She went and brought cold meats, white bread, and dried fruits on a shiny tin platter and placed them on the table along with a silver beaker of wine.

After the meal ended, the stranger began: "My name is David and I come from a large and celebrated trading city on the Baltic behind whose walls and in whose houses great wealth and immeasurable riches are stored. My father was considered one of the most powerful merchants in the city. His ships plied every sea and his money sat in every bank. I was his sole heir, and since I was sufficiently worthy and honorable to continue his name to the next generation he betrothed me to the daughter of an equally respected business associate from Portugal. On the very day my wedding was arranged, the Almighty—blessed be His name!—determined a different fate for me and that my hopes should come to naught. For three days in a row, messengers of ill arrived at my father's house. One bore a letter from my father's largest debtor in Lisbon. He described how he would never be able to pay his debt for he had lost all his property in a deal gone bad and had to flee to Africa in order to evade the hands of the law. The next one brought word of pirates in the South Atlantic who had plundered and burned a ship which was just returning from India laden with the majority of our money in silks and spices. Finally the third recounted how in the sea around Helgoland where there are innumerable sandbanks and hidden reefs a storm shattered the ship carrying the rest of our wealth in ready money. It had just left Amsterdam, the crown city of commerce, whence our business manager had sent the debts he had collected.

"The wealthy merchant from Lisbon received word of my father's misfortune in the harbor of a city on the French coast, just as he was about to marry off his daughter to me. He turned right back around and wrote to my father, repudiating the engagement and declaring that neither I nor his daughter were any longer bound by the pledge.

"But the misfortunes were not yet exhausted. My father's loss was more that he could bear. The judges sold our house and garden and all of our expensive tapestries and furniture. As if all of this were not enough, they locked my father up in the deepest dungeon of the debtor's prison. There he was to languish till someone might volunteer to pay his debt or go his bail, or until death should take pity on him and settle the accounts.

"Not only did they throw me out of my childhood home, but they drove me from the gates of my native town. I went door to door to the houses of my father's friends, but they neither wanted to listen to me nor know me. I reproached them, reminding them that my father had always stood by them in similar times.

"I set off to wander the wide world, to earn my bread and seek relief and redemption for my hapless father. I have roamed across many countries and have seen many cities; I have gotten to know many peoples but have found no one to take pity on me and my father. I have told my tale in the hovels of the poor and the houses of the rich. Their hearts were moved, their tongues condoled, their lips consoled me, but no hand was lifted to help me.

"After some weeks I came to your country. When I arrived, everyone spoke of Rabbi Baruch the Cantor, praising his singing and extolling his virtuosic skill on the fiddle. From that moment it was my most fervent desire—next to redeeming my father—to come to know a man of such renown and spend some time in his company. In better times I too devoted myself to song and fiddle-playing, loving art above all things. So I permitted myself no rest and wandered day and night till I learned where you lived and could step inside your house.

"So now you see me here before you; you know my name and where I come from. But it is my most ardent wish that you permit me to learn from you and that you take me on as one of your songsters. I will gladly serve you and promise to obey you in all things, as you wish. Perhaps at your side I might develop into a skillful cantor and return with honor to my native town with sufficient earnings to redeem my father."

Rabbi Baruch listened attentively to the stranger, and Genenda felt sincere pity for this man who at such a young age had endured so remarkable and woeful a fate.

Now that he understood what the stranger wanted, Rabbi Baruch stood, picked up his large prayer book, and instructed him to recite and chant various passages by way of examination. Finding that David knew how to read in a clear, intelligible way and that his voice had a pious tone, he said to him: "David, you shall be one of my songsters! There is much, indeed nearly everything, that you must learn. You seem not to be so practiced in the traditional style of singing. But you are industrious and attentive and well-intentioned, so you might well soon become a good singer."

Rabbi Baruch and the stranger went to the synagogue to recite Minchah. In the twilightening period between

Minchah and Ma'ariv they continued to talk until the stars appeared in the sky, signaling the beginning of the evening prayers and the end of the Sabbath. The stranger took his leave of Rabbi Baruch, promising that on the eve of every Sabbath and festival from then on he would come to the Rabbi's house in order to learn how to sing, but that on the weekdays he would go about the country in search of employment.

The next morning, Rabbi Baruch arose early and gathered his fiddle and his songsters. He blessed Genenda and they set out beyond the distant mountains as that evening they were to sing and play at the castle of an esteemed knight, many miles away.

Genenda was left alone in the little house. She was used to spending such times either taking care of small household chores or in preparing sumptuous and inventive embroideries in silk and gold. Orders came from near and far when someone wished to dedicate an ark curtain or a Torah mantle for a synagogue. From time to time her playmates would come over in the evening and tell each other stories and sing songs, as was their way.

That week, however, neither her work nor her songs were much of a success. She often sat alone for hours at a time brooding, though she knew not over what, and feeling sad, though she had no idea why. When her friends were absent for some time, she was impatient; and when they did visit her, she remained silent, telling none of the many stories she knew, nor singing songs with them, though she had the finest voice of them all. When one of the girls started singing a song and then another chimed in, and then another, and finally all of them together—her dark eyes moistened and her sweet voice resounded with a marvelous brightness as if she were trying to sing into her own beautiful, brimming soul. The girls exulted at the song and said it had never sounded as lovely.

So the week passed till Friday came again. At an hour after noon Rabbi Baruch returned to Genenda and his community. And after him the new singer arrived as well.

While all week long Genenda had been taciturn, pale, and sad, now she danced cheerfully around her room and into the little garden behind the house. She sang once again as an indescribably sweet redness flushed her cheeks. Rabbi Baruch, whom she had been deprived of for so long and whom she loved so dearly, was now with her once more. She hastened to spread the dazzling white cloths over the table and sideboard, scatter light-colored sand on the polished floor, and braid the seven wicks for the Sabbath candlestick.

Rabbi Baruch meantime busied himself with teaching the new singer the tune for the hymn "Lecha Dodi," for that evening at the Sabbath eve service in the synagogue was to be his first time singing with them. He brought a harp with him, and just as quickly as he caught the singular beauty of the tune and learned how to sing it he was also able to devise an equally beautiful accompaniment for it on the harp. Rabbi Baruch was overjoyed at his keenly intelligent pupil and heaped praise upon him.

When Rabbi Baruch stood before the ark and began leading his singers in "Lecha Dodi"[6] the voice of the new singer sounded singularly holy compared to the others—like the bells ringing in Christian churches; and his harp rang out with unaccustomed solemnity between the verses of the song—like the reverberations of a Cathedral organ. A profound silence reigned in every corner of the synagogue; not a breath stirred. All were gripped by the heavenly harmony of Rabbi Baruch and his singers as they stood in deep pious devotion.

Such it was on every subsequent Sabbath. The new singer's voice was splendid. He was soon able to sing all the prayers, indeed probably better than any singer ever could.

The "Great Sabbath,"[7] finally arrived. All of the songs in praise of God, the Liberator from the shackles of slavery, sounded as majestic and beautiful as they must have in Solomon's Temple. "David!" Rabbi Baruch said to the new singer. "Truly a second David, a new star of song has risen for Israel!" He hugged and kissed him, and Genenda was beside herself with joy as if it were *she* her father was embracing. "Genenda!" he said to her. "A new king has arisen in Israel and you are his queen!"

Passover arrived. On the first night Rabbi Baruch sat in a soft, padded armchair, dressed in white graveclothes, for it was on this night the firstborn of Egypt perished while the firstborn of Israel survived. On the side-tables to his right and left, and on the table in front of him, stood treasures of silver, vessels of gold, and expensive raiment, for on this night every son of Israel is to feel like a king. On this night the children of Jacob went forth out of the land of slavery and were set free. In doing so, God, the king of kings, crowned his people with the most beautiful crown of nations—Freedom.

By his side sat David, the dear one of his soul, and Genenda, the darling of his heart. Both festively adorned, they sat across from one another. In a loud voice Rabbi Baruch recounted the children of Jacob's years of suffering in Mitsrayim,[8] and David and Genenda followed along, accompanying him in occasional antiphons to the Lord.

When the Haggadah[9] had concluded and they had tasted the Bread of Affliction and the Bitter Herbs[10] and the wine David arose, walked up to Rabbi Baruch, and addressed him: "Rabbi Baruch. You know how I have become estranged from my homeland. My father, the only one who still bound me to that place, has passed on home to his ancestors. Your home, however, is to me another homeland; you have yourself become a second father to me. You have accepted me and instructed me in the high art of song and given me hope that one day I might be worthy of being the finest cantor alive today. Along with that hope you gave me the reassurance that I shall not have to starve for as long as I live. For the art of singing is a holy art and sustains abundantly those who practice it with love and dedication.

"You have already done me so many kindnesses, but let me ask you for one more! Let your singer become your son. Give me Genenda for a wife!"

David's words came unexpectedly to Rabbi Baruch. He considered before he spoke so as not to say anything rash or do anything hasty.

He looked at Genenda and noticed how at the young man's words her cheeks blushed deeply and reflected the ethereal light of modest maidenhood as they used to only at dawn on an early spring morning. His searching eyes noticed how she had cast her eyes down and how her white fingers toyed with the abundant dark locks that tumbled freely down her neck, over her shoulders, and onto her bosom. He lovingly took her chin and asked, "Genenda, my daughter, as David has asked for you to be his wife, do you wish to follow him?"

Genenda, however, said neither yes nor no. She simply looked at Rabbi Baruch with her large, dark eyes. He saw a bright tear glistening in them and understood.

He turned to David and said, "Genenda will be your wife, if you can continue to prove yourself a skillful singer. But know that as I am giving her to you for a wife, she is *all* you will get. Genenda is Genenda's dowry!

"It is written in the Holy Law: a woman will leave her father and her mother to follow her husband and cleave to him; the husband, though, will love his wife and sustain her and be in place of her father and mother. So shall you also do. But first you must be able to earn enough to support her, and you must prove that you can."

When Rabbi Baruch finished, David replied: "Let singing and harp playing be my bread because it is yours. I will do what you do and will travel around with my harp; but I will not travel on the same path. When you go right I shall go left, and when you turn left I shall turn right. And whatever I earn I shall bring to you each week so that you will see that David deserves Genenda. But because the union we are about to conclude is such a holy one, let us consecrate it on this holiest of nights!" At these words he drew a ring from his finger and slipped it onto the ring finger of Genenda's right hand,[11] reciting: "With this ring I consecrate you as my wife for all time according to the law of Moses and Israel!" Rabbi Baruch said, "Amen!"

Afterwards the three new family members held a lavish feast to celebrate. After much discussion it was settled that once the holiday ended David should give Rabbi Baruch a letter in which he promised, according to tradition, to pay 400 florins to the bride if for whatever reason he wished to renounce the marriage. In return David was to receive from Rabbi Baruch a letter in which he pledged, forever and always, to abjure the title of Cantor, and in general never to sing or wield a bow again should he go back on his promise and deny him Genenda for a wife. And it was further settled that the wedding should be celebrated on Sabbath Nachamu[12]—a Sabbath of consolation and joy.

The eight days of Passover proceeded joyously and on the day after the holiday the letters were written. David parted from his father-in-law and from his bride and gave his word to return on the coming Friday with his weekly earnings.

When Friday came, he did return and poured out a great quantity of gold and silver onto Rabbi Baruch's table. Rabbi Baruch was astonished, for he had not played or sung as much in a year as David had in the first week of his being a singer.

The same happened on every subsequent Friday. David gave the money to Genenda that she might save it up as her own property. He also brought her expensive jewelry of gold and precious stones and many clothes of velvet and costly embroidery. For he loved her exceedingly and she loved him as she only loved her father—and likely more so.

Meantime, Sabbath *Nachamu* approached, and Rabbi Baruch was busy making arrangements for the wedding of his beloved only daughter. Soon all was ready, with a feast provisioned worthy of a rich and famous cantor. The guests had been invited, and singers and musicians were gathering from far and wide to exalt Genenda's wedding.

However, when the Sabbath finally arrived and the girls had gathered around Genenda in the Rabbi's house and all the boys were standing outside the door waiting to greet the groom and congratulate him, in his place came a messenger carrying a letter from David's hand. He wrote that because of an important piece of business it would be impossible for him to arrive on Friday. Since he did not wish to profane the Sabbath by traveling, he would arrive first thing Sunday morning; no one should be troubled, and everything should remain prepared as it was. The news distressed Genenda greatly and she cried amongst her playmates. But when she saw the letter and recognized David's writing she was consoled and grew merry once more. On the last day of her maidenhood she played and sang with her playmates and was happy again.

That night, however, she spent sleeplessly in her room. She could find no rest on her bed nor joy in her Psalter, where she had once been so easily edified, because she was thinking about David, about what he was doing and where he had been delayed.

The girls returned in the morning to braid her lovely, long, shiny black hair into wide plaits and wove a string of pearls into the braids. They freshened her white dress and put her white veil on, singing songs for her departing youth and for the mirth and lightheartedness of an unbound heart. Then they led Genenda into the main room, which had been transformed overnight into a festively decorated hall, and seated her on a throne with white-silk cushions behind rustling green-silk curtains. They took their places on either side of her in a half-moon around the throne. Music started up behind the doors and the women entered in pairs, dressed in rich gold bonnets and long flowing dresses. Each carried two silver cymbals. They struck them together so that they rang out in unison, bright and splendid. Then they began dancing before the girl on the throne to the sound of the cymbals. They danced and brandished wreaths; the dance looked like a battle for the bride whose outcome would determine whether the bride would belong to the women or remain with the girls.

At last the girls yielded to the women's cymbals and circled round the throne. One of them stepped up to Genenda and removed the veil from her locks and the pearls from her braid; with a pair of golden shears they cut off her lovely, long, raven-black hair, which fell to the ground. The girls brought the locks and the braid to Genenda as a remembrance that they had once been playmates. Genenda, however, grew pale and wept softly. The Rabbi of the congregation entered, grave and formal, followed only by his servant, for apart from him no man was supposed to set foot in the bride's chamber. He approached Genenda solemnly and set a green silk veil, trimmed with thick gold lace, over her head and face. He blessed her softly and left as grave and formal as he had come. Now the men were permitted to enter and they gathered around Rabbi Baruch in the bride's chamber and inquired after the groom. But he still had not arrived and they were beginning to worry.

The bright sounds of trumpets and shawms pealed outside, and the stamping of many steeds' hooves could be heard. The door flew open and in strode a stately young man in the bright, lustrous attire of a knight. It was David. Everyone recognized him; fear and astonishment in equal measure stopped the tongues of everyone present.

The knight, however, walked free and haughty among the men and, turning to Rabbi Baruch, said, "I am come to celebrate my marriage to Genenda and I am here to take her back with me to my house. Let her follow me! She has been wedded to me by the word which you gave me, and she is mine by her own free will. For that reason I demand her!"

Thus spoke the knight and he made to near the throne on which Genenda was seated in wondrous beauty but pale with her heart's anguish. Rabbi Baruch rushed to block his way and stood frantically before the throne. He thrust him back and cried out with a voice trembling with rage, "Begone! You shall not have Genenda! I did not father her for a son of Ishmael nor did I raise her for a son of Esau!"

"So you are denying me what you swore to me before God and what is mine according to the Law of Moses and Israel? A law which you and she obey and to which I submitted when I took Genenda as a wife? I could compel you by force, as a hundred soldiers have followed me here and are awaiting my signal. But I do not wish to take Genenda by force since she is mine by right and by her own heart. So let her reach her hand out to me to follow me in peace to be my wife, for that is what she is!"

He tried once more to approach the throne, but Rabbi Baruch pushed him back more furiously than before as Genenda buried her face in the cushion of the throne and wept.

The knight strode into the middle of the assembly and cried out, "You are all witnesses that Rabbi Baruch the Cantor has desecrated the Word of God and has violated the law! So know this: he does not deserve to stand before the Holy Ark nor is he worthy to lead the community of Jacob in prayer. For he is an oathbreaker and a blasphemer. He has laid this anathema upon himself by denying Genenda to me as a wife!"

Having spoken, the knight strode out and rode swiftly away with his hundred soldiers.

In Rabbi Baruch's house dismay and deep sadness reigned. Only a few tried to comfort the deeply shaken cantor or console the miserable bride. The guests quietly lost themselves in one another's sorrow.

The day passed and night came. Rabbi Baruch hurried out of the house of mourning to wander about on the banks of the river and among the cliffs of the Vyšehrad and further up the limestone crags, pouring forth his heart's laments into the night and weeping to the stones the song of his soul. Not till late in the morning did he return to his house. Genenda was still sitting on the throne, her face hidden in the white silk cushion, wet with tears. On the ground lay her long, beautiful, raven locks, her braids, and her veil. The girls had wanted to take no memory of such grief and sadness with them when they left Genenda's house.

He lifted her up and wrapped her in his arms, kissing her and speaking words of consolation. She calmed down. Her comforter was indeed her father and, other than David, the only person she loved in the world. Yet she would no longer be happy, wandering silently around the house like a widow, wearing mourning clothes. The girls no longer came to visit for she was taken for a widow.

Rabbi Baruch, too, became taciturn. He no longer derived any joy from song or bowstring, and his fiddle hung on the wall, covered in dust. The singers forswore his company for he was no longer considered a cantor, and no more did he wander the country singing and playing. He had imposed this excommunication on himself.

So the days passed in pain and the weeks in sadness at the house of Rabbi Baruch the Cantor.

It was on the Sabbath blessing the New Moon of the month of Elul[13] in late August when a messenger arrived, bursting into Rabbi Baruch's house and handing him a long letter from the king's hand. In it Rabbi Baruch, referred to as "the Cantor," was informed that in three days' time he was to appear in the hall of the High Court in the stronghold of the Vyšehrad. Should he fail to arrive on the appointed day and at the appointed time judgment would be rendered in favor of the plaintiff.

Genenda was not at home when the messenger came. She had gone to the riverbank to be alone as she so often used to do. When she returned home Rabbi Baruch told her that in three days he would be going on a journey and wasn't sure when he would return. He concealed from her the messenger's visit and the order for his appearance at the king's High Court in the Vyšehrad.

Rabbi Baruch spent those three days in the entrance hall of the synagogue, sitting on the floor, fasting and praying like a penitent. On the third day he dressed in his holiday finery, put on his black silk coat, and donned his smooth, round skullcap. He blessed Genenda with the blessing made over loved ones when departing on a journey from which one's return is unsure. He then took up his walking stick and set off for the fortress of the Vyšehrad.

He arrived precisely at the appointed hour and was led to the king in the hall of the High Court.

There the king sat in judgment upon his throne, with all his councilors and the nobles of his realm standing around him. Rabbi Baruch bowed low. The door on the opposite side of the chamber opened and the young knight entered as plaintiff and bent his knee to the king. The king signaled him to speak and he began:

"This man, Rabbi Baruch, known as the Cantor, has a daughter named Genenda. I saw her one evening at dusk as I was enjoying myself on the Moldau. There she was, strolling along the riverbank weaving garlands of rushes and willow leaves. My heart burned with love for this most beautiful maiden I had even seen in all my travels across the world. I alighted from my boat, hurried toward her, and greeted her in a friendly way. But she fled like a timid deer from a hunter and disappeared into one of the houses the Jews live in at the foot of the Vyšehrad. I returned to my boat and sailed home. But I could not get the image of the maiden out of my mind, and I swore to myself that she would become my wife. But the path of violence did not seem to me to be the way that such a love should proceed, so I decided to acquire it through peace. You, great King, were then pursuing war with your neighbors; I had to follow you, and I stood by you as you destroyed your enemies in the desolate forest on the border. When the war was over and we returned I went to Rabbi Baruch and became one of his singers. I lived with him according to his law as a Jew. When I discovered that Genenda returned my love I peaceably asked her father for his daughter's hand, and he promised her to me as a bride. I placed a golden ring on her finger and consecrated her as my own according to the law of Moses and Israel according to which I was then living. He said, 'Amen!' and gave me this letter as a proof and affirmation of this covenant. I then knew that Genenda was inviolably and irrevocably my wife—for she had accepted the ring without coercion and of her own free will, and this was my wife for the price of the ring. I left the faith of Israel and returned to the bosom of the church, doing penance as I had been enjoined and commanded. I then went to bring my wife home, to convert her in the arms of love, so that she would follow the faith of her husband and through love attain salvation in the faith of that love. Rabbi Baruch, however, refused me what was mine before God and man. So here I now stand as a plaintiff, claiming what is mine by right as is written in this letter written by him."

The king took the letter, but when he saw that it was written in Hebrew he summoned three Rabbis whom he kept at court for such cases. They each read the letter aloud and translated it for the king. Once the king had grasped the meaning of the letter word for word he turned toward Rabbi Baruch and said, "Rabbi Baruch, you are by virtue of the law the defendant, and the law is on the side of the knight. Do you give him his wife and depart hence freely? Yet you have persisted in denying what is his and so you are forfeit in the punishment you have placed upon yourself. Since as an oathbreaker you are not to be trusted willingly to suffer your punishment and to forbear singing and playing; you shall thus remain imprisoned until such time as you desire to state before me, my nobles, and my councilors that you will give your daughter to this knight as a wife."

So spoke the king. Rabbi Baruch bowed low and replied, "It shall be as the king wishes, but my daughter will never become the wife of a man who believes in a faith other than that of the children of Israel!"

The king then turned to the knight and said, "Your right shall be yours! However, go forth on the path of Right to seek what is Right and refrain from all violence or force in seizing or abducting Genenda. Should you attempt one or the other you will have forfeited your right and the girl will again be this man's free daughter."

At that he signaled with his hand and the assembly dispersed. The young knight left the chamber and Rabbi Baruch was put in irons and led off to prison.

There he sat between the bare, damp walls, in the frost and darkness. No sunlight could penetrate the barred windows, unable to provide him any light or warmth. Only by the resonant striking of the tower clock above was he able to reckon the hours and by the weak, sallow reflection on the opposite wall could he measure the days. From time to time the iron trapdoor in the ceiling of the dungeon would open and the jailer would lower bread and water by chain. The jailer would tell him he was instructed to ask whether he intended to change his mind or not. Rabbi Baruch always replied, "It is not my intention nor will it ever be!" and the door would once again scrape shut. Days and weeks passed in this way in the desolate solitude of the dungeon while at home Genenda awaited him, not knowing what had happened to him, where he could be, or why he had sent her no message.

Four weeks passed and the holy month of the High Holidays arrived, the month of Tishre, the first day of which was celebrated as the first day of the New Year. On that day God created man after he had completed the creation of heaven and earth and all the other beings that fill it so that man might be the crown of His great work and the ornament of Creation and its Master. On that day God remembered His people, their transgressions and their suffering, and was merciful and gentle in judgment, for He discerned that much had been suffered and endured and that while man's sins on the earth were numerous, more numerous still were his sufferings.

Then came the ten days of repentance. The community gathered in the synagogue at midnight to sing penitential hymns till dawn. Then they said their morning prayers and fasted all day long, making solemn vows and performing acts of atonement until the stars appeared in the evening. They repeated these acts of repentance for nine days and on the ninth they dressed in their shrouds—man and woman, boy and girl—and assembled in their synagogue in the evening. They prayed and wept and confessed and beat their breasts for their sins. They did not break up that night nor on the following day till sunset. For it was the Sabbath of Sabbaths, the great Day of Atonement, Yom Kippur, on which it was determined in Heaven who would become rich and who would be made poor; who would be healthy and who would be sick; who would perish and who would be saved; who by fire, who by sword, who by water, who by storm, who by hunger, and who by pestilence; who should live and who should die. So God would grant clemency and mercy to Israel instead of strict judgment.

For the five days after the Yom Kippur the people everywhere built lightly constructed huts made of wicker and planks, called *sukkot*, in front of their houses. They draped the walls with tapestries and brightly colored fabrics and decked them with artistically wrought decorations of parchment and gilded wood. They covered the roofs with pine boughs and other foliage, but not so thickly that the pleasant light of the stars might not shine down through the branches as they sat together in the huts celebrating Sukkot, the Feast of Booths in commemoration both of their forefathers' forty-year-long sojourn under the open sky after their flight from Egypt and of God's shelter and protection. From the pine boughs they hung gilded fruit, bouquets of flowers, wreaths, and garlands in remembrance of the fact that the eight days of this holiday in Jerusalem were days of joy in the harvest and the blessings of plentiful vineyards.

Genenda, too, built a sukkah in front of Rabbi Baruch's house and decorated it like the others. She hung a seven-branch candelabrum which she lit on the first evening of the festival. She sat in the sukkah, dressed, for the first time since her widowhood, in festive garments, for it was a feast of universal joy in which the sadness of the individual was supposed to pass away. She awaited her father whom she expected to return during the holiday. But the first two days of the festival as well as the interim period passed and the groom had still not returned to his Genenda nor the father to his daughter. For there he lay in chains in the Vyšehrad fortress above and no one knew.

In the darkness he did not forget the Lord's holiday and prayed aloud and sang songs of lamentation into the quiet night so that the watchmen upon the walls might listen, understand, and be moved by the pained, melancholy singing; and that the king in his bedchamber might awaken from a dream in which he had been accused by an ill-treated angel before God, the king of kings and judge of judges, on the great day of judgement and atonement. There in his dungeon Rabbi Baruch celebrated Rosh ha-Shanah and the Day of Yom Kippur and Sukkot. He edified his heart in misery by communing with God, the refuge of the humbled, and braced his soul through his tears, the balm of the oppressed, as did Jeremiah on the ruins of Jerusalem, and Job on the rubble of his fortune. But he knew that Simchat Torah, the Feast of Rejoicing in the Law, was nearing—the most wonderful day in Israel's year, the day on which every breast might rejoice in boundless joy and the houses of worship resound with the cheers of the people; the day most beloved by Genenda and in which she delighted year after year, her father giving her gifts of numerous trinkets and permitting her to dance merry roundelays with her girlfriends. His heart gradually swelled as he pictured himself at home in his soft armchair with his happy child standing at his side, flattering him for lovely gifts. How he delighted along with Genenda in these lovely things! He pictured himself in the midst of his congregation heading the festive procession surrounded by his singers, carrying a Scroll of the Law wrapped in silk and gold; the rabbi of the congregation following him, surrounded by his acolytes with another Scroll; the rest of the men with burning torches; the boys with brightly colored banners below small lit wax tapers; and the girls in pairs with floral wreaths. After circling the dais three times they would process out into the open, through all the streets of the community. He would sing songs of rejoicing and every voice would join in a deep, loud Hosanna.

He sank powerless onto the cold marble to which he was chained and wept aloud; his spirit of patience was broken.

For all this was now lost to him, to be shunned for the rest of his life. He was no longer permitted to be cantor nor to stand before the Holy Ark. And he was separated from Genenda, his sole comfort.

Thus he lay there that night. And in the morning, when the trapdoor opened and the jailer lowered his bread and water by chain and asked him once again whether his mind remained unchanged, he gathered himself up off the floor and called out, "You have crushed my spirit and bruised my pride and rendered me a shadow of myself! I am left with but one support keeping me from wavering, from plunging off the path of salvation into the terrifying abyss of blasphemy—the faith of my fathers! I will sacrifice all to preserve that one thing. Take everything but leave me that! I came into the world with nothing and will live in it in poverty; God gave me a wife and child and took them back again. Take all that I have left—take Genenda—let her follow that fraudulent husband if that is her wish! Just let me hold onto my faith; allow me to follow its commandments, allow God's light to lead me out of this dark Egypt, out to my community, so that I might celebrate Simchat Torah with them!"

No sooner had he spoken these words than the jailer loosed his bonds and led him out of the dungeon. Before the king and in the presence of the nobles of the realm and the councilors of the land he repeated these words: "Let Genenda follow him if that is her wish!" He signed the words in a document written by the king's chancellor, and the king let him return to his Genenda.

He hurried down from the Vyšehrad to his house and entered, his heart pounding. Not finding Genenda within he rushed outside into the *sukkah* and saw Genenda sitting over her psalter praying for her father. Her eyes were red from continued weeping. "Genenda!" he called out. "My child!" But she hardly recognized him; his countenance was haggard and his eyes careworn, his beard was tangled and his holiday raiment in tatters. He enclosed her in his arms and she finally recognized her father by his kiss, clinging to his neck in the bliss of reunion. "Child," he said, "I've been deprived of you for so long; I've suffered and endured so much in that separation. But I suffered it gladly and it was not too much to bear because it was for you! Ready your bridal costume, for a man will come to bring you home, and if you wish to follow him, so shall you do!"

Genenda's cheeks blanched again at these words; her lips quivered as if pleading for mercy. But her father had commanded and she obeyed. She went inside and put on her bridal attire, and her jewelry, and all the valuable things she possessed and sat in the darkness while Rabbi Baruch went to the synagogue. Staring out at the blue river she wished with all her heart that their lives might have rushed past as swiftly as those waves.

And behold! There coming down the river, a strangely decorated ship. Red and white banners fluttered from the masts, the pennant-sails, and the railing. The hull was painted with brightly colored carnival figures. At the prow sat a man dressed in a thousand variegated patches pulling comic pranks and capering merrily. All the ropes were entwined with flowers, and boys and girls were dancing on the deck. From the highest mast above it all a large standard fluttered and emblazoned on it in gold letters was the name *Genenda*. Genenda's heart pounded at the sight of the ship for she knew what it portended. The ship landed on the bank in front of her father's house. A young knight alighted by cheerful leaps and in a moment lay at her feet. "David!" she cried out in horror and buried her face in her hands. In a sweetly fawning voice the knight asked, "Genenda, will you be mine?" She, however, turned away from him and retorted dismissively, "Never! I can never be yours. You are alien to my race so you must be alien to my heart!" The knight then showed her her father's written consent, signed by his own hand. He implored her with irresistibly tender words and wrapped his arm around her slender body, pointing toward the decorated ship as she followed him silently, her gaze downcast.

Loud rejoicing greeted her on the ship and was immediately returned by the cheers of the prankster on the prow and the sailors at the oars. To the bright singing of the boys and girls on the deck the ship swished back upriver the way it had come.

Genenda walked over to the ship's railing and as if by accident dropped the ring she had received from David into the water. To catch the ring as it fell she leaned quickly over and plunged into the flood facing the distant rocky slope of the Vyšehrad.

Screams of terror rushed from every corner of the ship, but it was too late.

After some moments, the oarsmen pulled Genenda from the bottom of the water and lay her upon the deck, on the azure silk couch that had been prepared as a seat of honor for her and the knight. She was pale and cold.

The ship turned round once again and landed in front of Rabbi Baruch's house. The girls from the ship bore the couch on which Genenda lay onto land and placed it with its beautiful corpse in the sukkah.

The knight signaled to the girls and they withdrew. He ordered the sailors to row the ship away. The banners no longer fluttered in the wind, but rather hung sadly from the pennant-sails as if weeping as the ship pulled away. The knight, however, remained behind, kneeling before the beloved corpse, silent in the depth of his pain. His searing grief had dried up the source of his tears.

Meantime, Rabbi Baruch was in the synagogue with his singers, leading his community in the celebration of Simchat Torah. In a hosanna no one had ever heard him intone so beatifically he poured forth the exuberant gratitude of his soul to God the Deliverer.

When he returned home, he walked into the *sukkah* and stopped on the threshold. There he saw Genenda, her eyes closed, laying wet, pale, and motionless on the azure silk couch, the knight kneeling at her side. He approached her quietly and touched her forehead. She was cold. He saw that she was dead and said in a trembling voice, "The Lord gave and the Lord hath taken away! Blessed be His name; blessed be the righteous Judge!"

He then went out to arrange for the burial of his daughter among the graves of the community of Israel.

That very night she was carried out on the azure silk couch and buried within the walls of the cemetery garden under an elder bush, for her death had been a sacrifice to sanctify and bless the name of God.

The next day in the synagogue Rabbi Baruch led prayers and sang with his singers the sublime songs of Zion as he had always done. For this was Simchat Torah.

Once the holiday had passed, however, he went into his house, locked the door, and rent his garments over the left breast. He strewed ashes over his head and sat in the dust on the floor for seven days and seven nights, reading Job and Jeremiah. He sang the Lamentations over Zion, the most beautiful of all beauties, which had fallen into dust and ruins, her ramparts sunk in ashes and her towers turned to firebrands. He then opened his house and went out again and lived as cantor of the community for many years. But his singing was only heard before the Holy Ark in praise of God, on the Sabbath and the three pilgrimage festivals, in Lamentation for the daughter of Zion on the Ninth of Av, and when he appeared before God as emissary of the community on the Day of Atonement. Nevermore did he wield a bow or sing a song of earthly joy.

The knight left Genenda's corpse to undertake a pilgrimage to Rome on foot to do penance. He was ordered to enter a monastery, so he returned home and sold his castle and all of his possessions. He distributed the redeemed money to the poor of Israel so that every year on the anniversary of Genenda's death, after the end of Simchat Torah, they would sing Psalms in her honor so that God might mercifully receive her into the flocks of those who died for the holiness of His name and that he too might be forgiven at the hour of his own death. He entered a monastery and served as lay-brother, bearing the name David till the end of this days.

Here Zerah went quiet. — — —

One evening Rabbi Cheskel, at whose school I was studying, slammed shut his large folio tome and said, "Children, pray your evening prayers and you may go home!" Tired from sitting for so long on the hard benches of the schoolroom we shut our well-thumbed books. Each of us picked up our prayer books, and stood facing the door over which hung the large plaque with the two golden lions holding the blue painted Star of David with the inscription:

East! From this direction blows the breath of God!

The eldest boy led the prayers and we followed along quietly as the sunset cast its red light over our books.

Once we had finished our prayers Rabbi Cheskel went into his rooms and the other boys snatched up their school bags and slates, noisily rushing out the door and thundering down the stairs. They chased each other along the narrow cemetery lane in cheerful abandon. I, however, stayed behind, walking over to the window and watching them until they had disappeared around the corner. Then I let my gaze drift over the old cemetery with its tangled elder bush, its long rows of mossy tombstones, and the mausoleums which had stood haphazardly among them since time immemorial, covered in century-old grasses and century-old neglect, and among which the pious and the faithful rest. How quiet everything was there! No breeze daring to disturb the greenery's repose and only the occasional faint stirring of a leaf, as if intoning a memorial prayer over the graves, or reading the half-worn inscription on a crumbling stone. Everything was as it had been yesterday, and the day before that, and the hundred years before that. As if nothing changed after death; as if eternity itself lay over these places of earthly peace.

But there was one thing my eyes sought today in vain: the old man with the silver beard and the tricorn hat, the faded gray smock and the long cane, the black silk stockings and the shoes with the silver buckles. That old man would often sit deep into the night before the door of the old, crumbling hut at the entrance to the cemetery. There he dwelt when he wasn't wandering among the tombstones, removing moss from the inscriptions or freshening them up with black varnish. The old man always seemed to me the soul of the cemetery incarnate, immortal as eternity, immutable as peace. These places of the dead seemed doubly dead to me today for he was not reviving them.

The strange glimmer of burning candles shone through the elder-clad windows of the hut and wrestled with the red of the evening the way a life flickering out does with awakening in the hereafter. I concluded that the man had stayed at home today, possibly engrossed in leafing through the lists of the dead from centuries past, as he enjoyed doing, in order to summon up the memory of the day of someone or other's death. They said he commemorated the anniversaries of the deaths of all the great rabbis. So maybe he was holding such a commemoration today and that's why the candles were burning.

In the meantime, it had grown dark. I sat down by the window, under the black bookcase, looking into the evening darkness of the gloomy house, and thought again of the old man from the old cemetery and all of the amazing things people told about him. I thought about how he had lived in solitude in that sinking hut for fifty years; how he never left but to make a tour of the cemetery; how he spoke to no one except Ensel, Rabbi Cheskel's assistant; and how he never had dealings with anyone but the lists of the dead and the gravestones.

The door opened and Ensel came in, sitting down silently next to me on the other seat by the window as he pulled his hat lower over his brow. When the moon rose and shone onto his face I saw him looking more serious than usual as he glanced over at the old man's hut and the windows emanating that strange light and the elder bushes that screened them. I asked him, "Ensel, do you know why the old man over there hasn't come out into the cemetery today and what the light shining in his window means?"

"My boy, the one I don't know," Ensel answered. "But as to the light, that I'll tell you. After evening prayers, I wanted to look in on the old man, but when I knocked on the door it wasn't opened for me. After knocking ten times and tugging on the latch in vain I finally put my eye to the keyhole and peered through. I saw the old man putting on his white shroud and his white skullcap, moving the high armchair in front of the window, lighting the wax candles, and placing them around the chair. He then picked up a book, sat in the chair, and started to pray. I recognized the book because I have borrowed it from him a hundred times when someone was to be buried or I was called to someone on his deathbed. It was the Ma'avar Yabok.[14] The light you now see is the light of those candles."

"Rabbi Ensel, what do you think it all means?" I asked again.

"Tomorrow is the Ninth of Av,[15] and the old man always celebrates it in his own way. Several years ago, he told me there would be a Ninth of Av coming which he would celebrate with particular solemnity and untold mournfulness. Perhaps tomorrow is the day the old man has long awaited."

"And is everything they say about him true?"

"Some is true and some invented. For those that knew the old man's history and fate now lie over yonder long since; and all that's left are but opinions and speculation from what is seen of him from day to day. The old man's actual story, however, is known to no living soul on earth apart from me. So that it may not sink into oblivion when eventually I am buried I will tell it to you."

At this Ensel put his chair in order, looking over at the light once more, and began:

In olden times the hut where the old man now lives was the charnel house for the first cemetery. There the dead were washed, laid out, and sanctified before burial. After the last corpse was buried in this cemetery and the Community had designated a new one outside of the city, the old man—the former beadle at the Old New Synagogue[16]—took possession of it and dwelt there ever since, withdrawn from the world, silent and solitary, as you yourself know. I was still a boy of about ten years old when the old man moved in. He quite enjoyed it when I came to visit him in his somber room still cluttered with the boards and barrels for washing the dead as well as the biers, shovels, and other such gear. I helped him out in many ways, such as bringing him charitable gifts that the wealthy donated, fresh fruit, and many other things that might make the gloomy places of the dead more comfortable. In return I heard from his mouth many strange tales of long forgotten times and people past recall, including his own amazing fate.

Once upon the Friday evening of the Sabbath preceding the Ninth of Av, when people prepared themselves for mourning Zion's fall and Jerusalem's destruction, the cantor of the Old New Synagogue chanted the benediction over the wine and the service came to an end. The congregation left the synagogue to announce in their homes and among their families the Sabbath that had just begun.

Numerous people stood on either side of the doorway and along the steps to the entrance hall leading from the depths of the house of worship to the open street. These were the orchim[17]—the poor strangers waiting for the householders who had invited them as guests to their houses for the Sabbath. There were also those who had arrived in town late on the evening before the start of the Sabbath who were now waiting anxiously to see whether someone leaving the synagogue might invite them to their table.

Those who had already been provided for gave their hosts the Sabbath greeting and went off with them. Nor were the latecomers left standing. Hospitable men took an interest in them and bid them in God's name to come along home with them.

On the bottom step, however, stood one *orach* whom no one had invited and to whom none of those leaving the synagogue had extended a hand in greeting. For he stood off to the side and his eyes did not range over them pitiably. His speech made no wheedling impositions. Everyone noticed him because his appearance was so strange as he stood on the bottom step in a tattered gray robe, leaning on a staff whose foliage was still fresh and green as if it had been plucked from a tree that very day. His snow-white beard fell down to his belt, and from both temples from under his broad, dusty hat hung snow-white curls down to his knees. With his unmoving face trained on the inside of the synagogue he fixed his sparkling gaze on the dark walls, a lustrous tear hanging in his eyelashes as if he were thinking of days long past.

When at last the rest of the congregation had left, Rabbi Wolf—the beadle and now the inhabitant of the old charnel house over there—once again made his rounds of the synagogue to check whether anyone had tarried in his prayers. He then made his way back to the entrance hall and looked around there as well before locking up.

That's when he noticed the curious stranger.

"Why are you lingering when everyone else has gone?" he asked him. "Have you not finished your Sabbath prayers? Then I'll wait till you're done. Or are you an *orach* who has not found a host? Well, if so then in God's name welcome and come with me. I am admittedly a poor man with neither wife nor children, but think of how even Abraham entertained the angel under the tree, and come along."

The stranger bowed his head and extended his hand silently to the beadle. The two left and Rabbi Wolf led his guest through the quiet streets, at once calm and peaceful from the Sabbath celebration and bright from the thousand little flames in Sabbath lamps shining through curtained windows into the still of a Friday evening. Girls darted out and back, and children impatiently awaited the blessing of returning fathers.

In pious custom Rabbi Wolf greeted the housewives standing in front of their doors, while his guest looked questioningly at the old decaying houses and then the newly built ones as if looking for something he could not find.

Near the old charnel house, in the same place where the tall new house now stands, then stood a small squat hut with a high wooden roof and a wooden porch. Rabbi Wolf opened the door and lead his guest through the dark corridor and into the main room, illuminated for the Sabbath.

However, before entering he touched the doorpost and recited the customary prayer, which every householder intones when entering or leaving his home, and which every stranger should do when staying as a guest.

He then stretched out his hands in the direction of the seven-branched lamp and softly said the blessing of the candles—which he had to do himself as he had no wife to do so. He sat down at the table covered with the white tablecloth on which a meager meal was already laid out and said to his guest, "Sit down by me, dear *orach*, and set aside your walking stick, for as it is written: 'When the Sabbath comes then comes rest'; and the stick, the instrument of wandering, is ill suited to rest."

The *orach*, however, had already stepped inside without touching the doorpost or giving the Sabbath greeting. He neither set aside his walking stick nor took his place as

Rabbi Wolf had bidden him but rather walked over to the window and stared silently out into the moonlit night.

"Tell me, my host," he said at last, turning to Rabbi Wolf, "is that not the cemetery out there where the moonlight shines?"

"It is," replied Rabbi Wolf. "But I would rather you seek your peace under my roof and take part in the Sabbath rest here with me. For you seem to have come a long way, a stranger in our land, and not for pleasure and amusement. You will need rest above all else."

"I have indeed come from a distant land," the *orach* responded, "a land which neither you nor any mortal knows. And my journey is indeed not one of pleasure. After all, I am not a stranger here but am rather, like you, a scion of the holy community of Prague. Let that suffice and don't importune me further with questions. But tell me, what is the meaning of that open grave there, the one the moon is shining into so brightly that one can count the pebbles at the bottom? Is it meant for a dead man whom you have neglected to bury today? Or is it your custom to keep graves dug at the ready since evil spirits wait impatiently for departed souls?"

"Neither!" Rabbi Wolf informed him. "That is the grave of an acher[18] in Israel, a Jewish heretic, that has lain open for half a century. Neither snow nor rain falls into it, neither dew nor frost; no grass grows on its edges, and birds avoid it as they fly lest they fall dead into it. It is the grave of the heretic Jehuda who disappeared so mysteriously from the earth and about whom so many amazing stories are told."

"Jehuda did you say?" the stranger asked. "And amazing stories are told about him? The Lord does indeed perform miracles. But what the eyes of men see is but the rough, impenetrable shell. The kernel is kindness and wisdom. Tell me, what do people say about Jehuda?"

"Many long years ago there lived here in Prague a bachur,"[19] Rabbi Wolf began eagerly, "by the name of Jehuda who had a reputation far and wide for uncommon erudition. He was the student of Rabbi Meir, who was then the head of the beit din,[20] the Rabbinical court. Rabbi Meir, recognizing in Jehuda a young man of singularly keen intellect, regarded him more as a colleague than a student. They studied and disputed, spending day and night together exploring the depths of the Holy Word.

"When Jehuda turned eighteen, Rabbi Meir said to him, 'If you continue as you have begun, then you will be proof of the promise that there will arise in Israel a man who will surpass Moses and whose name will be borne from one end of the world to the other and whose renown will reach as far as wherever the one God is known.' Jehuda, however, replied, "Yes, I do wish to prove the promise true! When God gave the tablets of the Law to Moses, He passed by unseen in the draft of the east wind. I, however, want to look at Him eye to eye and face to face. For in wisdom lie the judgments that banish even God! I will ask Him questions that Moses failed to ask, on account of which Israel now wails in servitude and in misery!' He then burrowed more deeply into the secrets of the Kabbalah, which had opened his spirit so early on.

When a year had passed Jehuda said to Rabbi Meir, "Rabbi, allow me to speak to the congregation from the stairs to the Ark!"

Rabbi Meir permitted him, and Jehuda gave his first sermon on the Sabbath before the Ninth of Av. Scriptural experts streamed in from every corner of the country so that the Old New Synagogue could scarcely contain them and the mass of people who had come to listen to Jehuda's oration.

"May the Lord protect your spirit," Rabbi Meir said to Jehuda after the sermon was over. "You've surpassed me at such a young age! One day to you was as seventy years to me. I now call you my master. How can I prove to you that my mouth says what my soul is thinking? So be it."

"Rabbi," Jehuda replied, "you have a daughter the equal of Rebecca in beauty and Rachel in kindness. Let me be your son, not only in word and spirit, but also in blood. Give her to me as a wife!"

"It will be as you wish," Rabbi Meir answered. In a few weeks' time he invited friends and relative to his house, and Malke, his only child, became Jehuda's wife.

After another year had passed and it came time for the Sabbath preceding the Ninth of Av, Jehuda turned suddenly taciturn and grave. He spoke neither to Rabbi Meir nor to his wife; he simply shut himself up in his study and studied day and night. He intended to give a sermon that Sabbath to confirm the promise of a man who would surpass Moses. Word of the sermon had already made its way to every community, and the learned Rabbis and scriptural scholars came to hear this man.

On the Friday evening before the appointed Sabbath Jehuda appeared in the Old New Synagogue. Rabbi Meir took his seat to his left, for, as he had said, "You are my master!" All eyes were upon Jehuda from whose lips the words would flow the next day, words that would sound more perfect than the word of Moses and penetrate more deeply the spirit of the Lord.

Here too, however, Jehuda spoke with no one. For the Kabbalah demanded that whoever wishes to see God face to face must for a certain period of time refrain from all earthly intercourse and conversation. He left the synagogue and returned home, silently blessing the wine and bread. He then picked up his gray robe and walking stick and prepared to leave.

His wife stepped up to him, her baby—Jehuda's first-born and only son—at her breast. "Rabbi," she said, "where are you going on the Sabbath with those peculiar clothes?"

Jehuda made no reply. Rather, he silently lay his hands upon the head of the child, blessing him in his thoughts, and also blessing his wife, and then he left. He walked in silence along the dark streets, for the Sabbath lamps had all gone out and no living soul was out walking among the houses.

He finally stopped in front of a dark gate, took a small book out from his breast pocket, and read from it a prayer whose amazingly intricate words contained the name of the ineffable. Three times he struck three hammer blows on the gate. "Who are you?" came a voice from within.

Jehuda answered, "I am Jehuda, the son of Naphtali, the son of Benjamin, of the tribe of Levites whence descended Moses the Teacher and David the King and Bard!"

"If you come from the tribe of Levites and acknowledge the teaching of Moses then why do you call him merely Moses the Teacher and not Moses *our* Teacher as it is written and as every other professing Jew does?" asked the voice.

"Because nothing that lived is unsurpassable," Jehuda replied. "And because between the lines of the secret books it is promised that one day a man shall arise who will surpass Moses!"

"So you question the divinity of Moses?"

"It is not the divinity of his words that I question," Jehuda answered, "but rather that he completely revealed to us the essence of God. That is why I want to see God myself and have come to this gate and demand entrance."

"Then turn to the writings of the wise men that explain his words," said the voice. "Seek the traces of their footsteps and you shall reach the same goal they reached!"

"I undertook that well before you advised me to! Moses' words are insufficient; all my study of them has brought confusion and obscurity. I no longer wish to wander in this darkness. I have returned to Moses himself and wish to continue where he left off. What he concealed I wish to make known, and that is why I want to see God face to face—but not as Moses saw Him, in the waft of the east wind! And that is why I have knocked on this gate and demand that it be opened!"

At that he once again struck thrice three hammer blows on the gate. It opened and, once Jehuda had entered, shut again behind him with a deafening noise. Jehuda looked around for the doorkeeper who had spoken with him, but he was nowhere to be seen. As far as his vision extended he saw only tombstones and green hills. He had found himself in the old cemetery. The repose of death lay all around the graves and bushes.

Jehuda laid his walking stick down in front of him and made his way around the wall, along the narrow footpath, which led to the oldest graves. For that is what he imagined he had to do to find what he was looking for. When he had made his way past the oldest graves and started working his way around the newer ones, he saw a figure seated on one of the tombstones, pale and motionless, completely wrapped in white robes like the ones used to clothe the dead.

When he noticed the figure, he stood still, in order to see who it was and what it might undertake to do.

As it happened, the figure rose, approached, and addressed him, "Jehuda, son of Naphtali, why do you pause in your progress? Do you hesitate when you have gone so far? And if you are not hesitating, then say what it is you seek in this abode of peace that you should disturb the repose of the Sabbath of Sabbaths."

"Are you able to answer my questions?" Jehuda replied. "If not, then let me go on my way. You are not God."

"I certainly am not God!" the figure said. "But there are many things I can explain. I am the first gravedigger of this cemetery. And though dead for more than a thousand years I have not ceased being watchman of this place. From child to old man I know where each and every person buried here lies, and who will yet be buried here and in which place!"

"Well then!" Jehuda said excitedly. "Show me the place that is destined one day to receive me, for that is what I seek and that is what I must find!"

The figure countered, "As a rule, you living only seek the places where your relatives lie so you can visit them and pray for them. Why are you looking for your own grave?"

"Is the grave not the doorway one struggles to get through out of this life and into another?" Jehuda asked. "And if that is so, then a living person must struggle through this gate to glimpse into eternity and behold God ruling in truth. I have the fortitude to behold Him more clearly than Moses dared. It is for that reason I wish to reach the gateway of my grave, living as I am; I feel within me the power to dare to inquire of God what He concealed from Moses."

"If that is so," the figure replied, "then step forward! Not far from the freshest area of the cemetery you will find the place you seek."

With that the figure disappeared behind one of the nearby bushes. Jehuda picked up his walking stick again and wandered every region of the cemetery until he had come to the last one, the one in which the most recently deceased lay buried.

After a few steps he seemed to see a stone rising out of the ground, shining white in the moonlight, on which was written:

Here lies Jehuda, the son of Naphtali,
Who wished to be more than Moses
And whom the hand of God led
Back through the future life to that of the past.

When Jehuda saw this he stepped up to the tombstone and tapped it three times with his stick all the while intoning the name of the mighty angels, taught only by the

Kabbalah. The tombstone tottered and the earth gave way under Jehuda's feet, swallowing him down and not closing back up again.

Meantime, Malke waited at home for her husband, passing the night in tearful anxiety. When people gathered the next morning at the Old New Synagogue to hear Jehuda's teaching—one which was to have surpassed the teaching of Moses in its wisdom—and Jehuda failed to appear, they went to his home.

"Where is the Rabbi?" they asked. "Does anybody know?"

"Yesterday, after the start of the Sabbath, he left with his robe and walking stick," Malke replied, crying. "And he has still not returned."

The gravekeeper, however, related how that night he had seen with his own eyes how a man had sunk into a grave, a man wearing a gray robe and carrying a walking stick. When they came to the cemetery to look for him, at the designated place they found an open grave. Ever since that Sabbath the grave has remained open; no snow falls into it in Winter and no rain in summer; no dew in the morning and no frost at night. No grass grows on its edges, and no birds fly overhead. And whoever walks through the cemetery avoids it, giving it a berth of ten paces.

Rabbi Meir, who had planted the vain audacity in Jehuda's soul, and Malke both grieved deeply, avoiding the eyes of the world. After a few months they were carried out and laid to rest not far from the open grave, as was the wish of both. What happened to the baby, though, that nobody knows. Since that time, no one has given much thought to the misfortunate child, whether it had somehow been taken care of and grown up or whether it had died in its young misery. But I do from time to time think of what kind of future the poor thing had, how friendless life may have been and how empty the world; whether he was destined to become a youth, an adult, or even an old man. For in the early hours of my existence I lost my own father and mother. I knew neither of them; I never even learned their names. I grew up in the guidance of unfamiliar hands—and truth be told, they were not the tenderest of hands."

With that Rabbi Wolf finished speaking.

The *orach* had been listening to him intently. "And you know nothing else of Jehuda's fate?" he asked, turning toward the beadle.

"What happens beyond the grave, no living person knows," he replied. "Nor is anything mortal known of Jehuda's story."

"Well then! I shall tell you what came to pass," the *orach* began. "The secrets of the hereafter, which God had concealed from Moses, Jehuda wanted to see. Is that not what you said? And indeed he beheld them, but to his sorrow and his humility! Where the human mind begins, there begins error. And curiosity is the germ of pride. Happy is he who walks the path of wisdom as far as the Lord designates through His servants, and who desires not to step beyond it, deviating neither to the right nor the left. The Lord, however, is merciful and benevolent, and in the hereafter only the hand of clemency, not of terror, holds sway.

The earth closed right over Jehuda's head, and wild thundering battered his senses all the while. He felt as though he were sinking through a bottomless void, deeper and deeper through darkness and driving storms. Above him he saw the earth's crust shrinking into the formless distances, gradually turning into arching clouds. Beneath him he heard a rushing like a thousand flowing springs and saw it dawning with indistinct shapes. The deeper he sank the clearer the shapes became to his vision, and he recognized rivers and lakes, mountains and valleys, forests and cities. When he finally felt firm ground again under his feet, he saw he was in the middle of a desolate moor, without neither hill nor tree, nor herb, grass, or spring as far as the eye could see. He didn't know where he was or where to turn, right or left, forward or backward.

After a long, wearying journey he finally caught sight of the battlements of a city jutting from a bosk of dark cypresses and shadowy cedars. Its denizens proceeded in pairs in long rows through the gates, clad in white robes, their faces pale and blissfully cheerful. They made their way through the city in festive procession, the men carrying lustrous Torah scrolls, the young men hymnals, and the women and maiden wreaths of white flowers. The children walked in pairs in front of them, carrying white pennons with sparkling stars. They all blissfully sang *Hosannah! Hosannah!* Jehuda saw them all walking through a dim, twilit doorway into a house, which in splendor and magnificence resembled none he had ever seen. He waited till the procession had gone by and then slipped in behind it into the house. The house, however, was the Temple of the Lord, and the festival they were celebrating was Simchat Torah, the Feast of Rejoicing in the Law.

After the singing of *hosannah* had finished, a young man climbed up to the Holy Ark and pulled aside the curtain, which looked as if it were completely covered with an embroidery of blue clouds and suns. He opened it and lifted out a Torah scroll, and the entire Temple was filled with a magnificent radiance. He sang, "This is the teaching that Moses established!" And the whole congregation joined in their assent. The young man, however, lay the Torah scroll down on a golden table, unrolled it, and in a clear voice recited the final section of Deuteronomy, the last Book of Moses. When he finished the verse: *And there arose not a prophet since in Israel like unto Moses!* the bard-king David stepped forth and sang it to the accompaniment of his harp, and the women in the adjoining hall joined in as well as the children on the steps to the Holy Ark. No lips in the entire Temple stayed quiet save those of Jehuda, for he could not join in praise of Moses. He left the Temple and hastened from the city, a city which seemed to him inhabited by beings who stood no closer to God than where Moses had stationed them through his teaching. He walked on undauntedly through wildernesses and wastes.

Weeks and months passed, and when another year had ended, he again saw in the distance the battlements of a city. When he entered the city, the inhabitants were again celebrating Simchat Torah, singing: *And there arose not a prophet since in Israel like unto Moses!* Again, Jehuda did not join in and set off once again on his pilgrimage.

He wandered thus for fifty years from city to city, and wherever he came people confessed in song: *And there arose not a prophet since in Israel like unto Moses!*

And when the fifty years had come to an end, he asked the gatekeeper of the last city in which he found himself, "Tell me, where can I find God that I might see him face to face?" And the gatekeeper answered him, "You have seen God beyond the grave, where people walk about in veils of dust; you have seen Him this side of the grave, as the souls walk, divested of dust and in full understanding. God lives in the lives of those who believe in Him, and among these you can find Him. Whoever seeks Him further than that, distances himself ever more from Him. For the Lord spoke to Moses as to no other mortal in life or after death; and no prophet shall arise in Israel like him!"

At which the gatekeeper discharged Jehuda from the city and once again he traversed steppes and moors, till one day he emerged suddenly from a gloomy ravine and beheld the blue sky and the green earth and, from a distance, the battlements of a city with a hundred towers. As he approached it he recognized it as the holy community of Prague, and it was the eve of the Sabbath preceding the Ninth of Av. He went to the Old New Synagogue and listened with mute vitiation to Moses being affirmed the one and only perceiver of

God. He tarried in the entrance hall until the beadle warned him that it was time to leave and took him home. The one you see here before you in the gray robe and the walking stick is Jehuda, the young man, the student of Rabbi Meir, the husband of the hapless Malke, the father of Baruch, the abandoned lad. His arrogance is broken; the veil taken from his soul; the scales removed from his eyes. He bears his fate contritely to wander the world till he has found what he set out seeking—his grave."

Astonished to the depths of his soul, Rabbi Wolf replied, "Jehuda! Is that really you? Like a miracle your words awaken in me the memory of the sad years of my earliest childhood, which I spent under the roof of the poorest man in the community. At that time, he named me Baruch. However, because 'Baruch' is the name of the 'blessed,' from early on no one much liked to call me that and instead they named me 'Wolf' due to the harshness of my fate. I myself forgot that I was once called Baruch, because I never was!"

When the orach heard this, he cried out in a loud voice, "Blessed be the righteous judge! Baruch, my son, it is at your feet I join in with all of Israel: the Lord is eternal and omnipotent, patient and merciful, and sincere; and no prophet shall arise in Israel like Moses!"

So said Jehuda, and these were his final words. He lay lifeless in the arms of Rabbi Wolf, his son; and Rabbi Wolf wept over the body of his father. That very night he rose and bore the body outside, laid it in the open grave, and raked earth into the grave. He did not return to his home, but rather went into the charnel house to mourn. He did not leave and has dwelt there to this very day. That is when the dead stopped being consecrated there and were brought outside the city walls instead. Yet upon Jehuda's grave fell snow and rain and dew and frost, and it became overgrown with swells of grass."

- - -

With that Ensel, Rabbi Cheskel's assistant, finished and looked over at the light of the candles glowing so wonderfully from the elder-clad windows of the old charnel house.

After a while he spoke again, "I have to look in over there," and left the house.

The next morning he returned and said, "The Ninth of Av, which Rabbi Wolf has awaited impatiently for so many years, has finally arrived. This afternoon at four o'clock he will be committed to the earth."

On the left bank of the Moldau, immediately facing Prague's old royal castle, there was a place where year in year out many black coals lay strewn among a heap of black stones, coals which neither all the waters of the Moldau, rushing by for centuries, nor the cloudbursts of summer were able to whitewash. It was also said that in the winter snow could not long remain on that place—it melted as soon as it fell. At such times that place with the black stones and the black coals against the wide white wintry expanse looked for all the world like an ink-stain in the middle of a clean sheet of fine stationery.

Long ago on that place there stood a house. The house belonged to a widow who lived there with only her one little daughter whose name was Blümchen.

The widow was a very capable and therefore much sought-after embroiderer in both silk and velvet. She worked only for the wealthy and was well paid for it. The queen had once come to her to have a costly, red-silk robe embroidered. This had enhanced her reputation and she never wanted for work. She and Blümchen lived happy and contented in their quiet and industrious seclusion. For nearly the whole year Blümchen never left the house for it contained all the comfort and joy that could be wished for.

When Blümchen turned sixteen, the widow, who was no longer young herself, began to worry about how best to secure her child's future.

One evening, having just finished an expensive piece of embroidery—a sumptuous curtain which a wealthy man had pledged to the Old New Synagogue—she fetched from her trunk a small bag of thalers she had been saving up for half her life. She poured them out on the table, counted them, and said, "Thank God, dearest Blümchen. It's not much, but a blessed bit of wealth! Now I can go looking for a suitor for you, and when I've found one who is suitably pious and learned and will love you, then…"

The widow didn't continue. Blümchen, however, rejoiced at hearing she should be getting a suitor, clapping her hands for joy and dancing around the room. She promised she would once more embroider as diligently as she had till then, which in turn delighted the widow who thought that would scarcely be possible.

The following evening, the widow went out and conferred with her friends about whether anyone knew of a suitor for her Blümchen; she was willing to offer a tidy sum for a dowry.

While the women in the street went back and forth, racking their brains to think of a choice suitor for Blümchen, our little one was sitting at home in the warm parlor by the well-heated stove—just as we are now—snug in the dusky evening light. Watching the red embers as they airily glimmered and sparkled, she couldn't get enough of the wondrous spectacle. As to what she was thinking about, that was nothing other than the suitor whom her mother would be bringing, and the wedding which would take place soon after, and how she would like to be a beautiful, proud wife just like the queen for whom she had only recently embroidered a red-velvet cloak. And as she looked into the fire and thought about all of this, for all the world she wanted to know what her suitor would look like.

She sat watching the embers for so long and with such yearning that eventually everything in them seemed alive—as if the coals were nothing but rose-gold palaces; as if the busiest of lackeys were bustling about in the loveliest courtyards, illuminated by radiant sunlight; as if the most beautiful ladies and handsomest lords were strolling in halls aglitter with polished rubies; as if all of this were happening for the sake of a single handsome young man lying on a divan of fiery red rose petals under a bower of perfect fire lilies in that most wonderful garden. A large book with fiery letters lay open before him, which he was reading so eagerly that he did not notice how the wisest rabbis with long snow-white beards, diadems upon their brows, and palm branches instead of scepters in their hands, walked past him, bowing silently, and how the most beautiful women, with sparkling diamonds in their headdresses and in their dark eyes, nodded to him in friendly greeting. He continued reading one page after another without interruption.

When the young man had finished reading the last page he closed the book, kissed the red-hot cover, and stood up. He left the bower and walked among the burning trees. Without looking either right or left at any of the people milling about and reverentially making way for him he left the garden and headed over fields and meadows straight for the bank of the Moldau and to the lonely house that stood there. He knocked on the door and said, "Open, lovely Blümchen! I have come for you; all the queens in the fiery garden and all the princesses in the ruby halls are less dear to me than you. You shall come away with me and live with me there in the garden, and they shall all envy you!"

As soon as the handsome young man left, however, the fiery garden began to darken. The beautiful figures milling about one after the other froze in place; the trees and fire lilies went extinguished; and the walls of gold and rubies collapsed. Only here and there came the fiery flash of the setting sun. Then all went dark, and there was nothing to see but a desolate heap of dead coals and ashes; nothing to hear but the monotonous lament of a familiar voice: "Blümchen! Blümchen! Where are you?"

This was the voice of the widow who had just come home and was not a little frightened to find the parlor dark and no Blümchen rushing out to greet her. Blümchen had not noticed that night had come and that the parlor had gone completely dark and that the fire in the stove had gone out. She had not given any thought to lighting the lamp. It felt like a dream to her when her mother came in and asked with an anxious voice, "Blümchen, where are you?"

After a while she managed to pull herself together. She rubbed her eyes, not knowing right away what had happened. She called out, still half dreaming, "Here I am, mother!" Hurrying over to the cupboard, she took out touchwood and flint and lit the lamp.

The widow, however, scolded her for having let the fire in the stove go out and said, "A girl who wishes soon to become a housewife must be mindful of the fire in the stove and the water in the barrel lest her husband have little expectation of peace. When I was sixteen, I had to manage an entire household with so much to do. But I could not let the fire in the stove go out. My mother would gladly have accepted the ill-fortune of my not finding a suitor!"

Blümchen kissed her mother and tearfully begged her forgiveness; she wanted to do no more harm and it would not happen again.

The widow went about preparing dinner. But she set about her task with such an earnest and yet calm expression, such an unusually serious and meditative look on her face that Blümchen might well think she had something else on her mind.

For a while she followed her mother with her eyes, as if wishing to ask: "Mother, are you still angry with me?"

Then all at once the girl felt she was no longer a child. Her heart pounded in her breast like a maiden suddenly in bloom and she grew very hot. Every time her mother came near and their eyes met, she cast her eyes down. She was afraid her mother would start talking at any moment, so she stood by the window and looked out into the white winter's night. She stared at the smooth coating of ice on the river which reflected the moon so mysteriously, as if it knew everything that she but dimly suspected. She tapped her little fingers against the windowpane flowered with frost and sang softly to herself:

Cinnamon and clove
In our garden grow.
Say how long, dear child, do,
Shall I yet wait for you?
Four flowers will be your gift
If you will be my wife;
Four flowers for the chuppah[21]
And sugar for the soup.

In the meantime, her mother had put the actual soup on the table. Blümchen sat down and both of them were silent for a while, pretending to eat.

Finally her mother spoke up, "You must now also learn how to make soup, Blümchen. You don't know how soon you might need to use it."

Blümchen blushed deeply at these words. She forced herself to smile but didn't respond.

The widow continued, "I have to see about what to do with that room over there. No one has stayed there since your blessed father died. We have to fix it up. One cannot know what may happen."

Blümchen acted as if she hadn't heard and looked down disconcertedly at the table.

The widow watched her for a while, as if silently scrutinizing what was going on in her child's heart. She brushed the lovely black hair away from the girl's brow and said, "Is it not true that Rabbi Feivel the goldsmith's son Jacob is a handsome young man? You know him! Of course, you were only a nine-year-old girl at his Bar-Mitzvah, but you danced with him and he gave you a whole bag of raisons and almonds. Rabbi Feivel's wife said you were just made for one another, and everyone there said so as well. Have you seen him since then? Oh, how he's turned into a splendid young man! There's no other who's as learned and lively and handsome, and such a capable goldsmith. At any moment he might take his seat in the Sanhedrin;[22] and should the king need a new crown, no one could make a lovelier one than he! Rabbi Ensel wants to set up a workshop for him, and you shall be his wife."

The widow fell silent.

Blümchen, however, who durst not open her eyes throughout the speech, was so startled she dropped her spoon.

The widow, remembering how startled she too had once been that she had also dropped a spoon, took it as a good sign. She got up from the table, kissed her daughter on both of her lovely eyes, and said, "He'll be coming next Sabbath. His father wants to make the visit with him so you might see one another. Be charmingly clever, dear Blümchen. You're sixteen years old after all, not a child anymore. You needn't wish to avoid what must come!"

Tears came to Blümchen's eyes.

The widow began to regret having spoken so much all at once to her child. Kissing her again she said, "That is why you are still my good child and will remain ever so! But now go to bed. Tomorrow when you get up, after you've slept on it, maybe we can talk some more."

But Blümchen said, "Mother, you see how childish I'm being!" With her beautiful white hands she wiped the tears from her eyes. She looked cheerful once again and skipped about the room. She stopped once more by the window, tapped her fingers against the pane, sang her little love song, and slipped into bed.

The widow laid her hands on Blümchen's head, blessed her, and said, "The eternal Watchman neither slumbers nor sleeps." She blew out the lamp and the little room went dark. In a few moments it was so still and quiet one might have believed the two had died. Only the silk bed curtains rustled furtively from time to time, and from behind them came the soft breaths of the slumberers.

Though it remained quiet the whole night—it was neither so peaceful nor so calm.

For Blümchen had scarcely fallen asleep when the spent embers in the oven came back to life. First a little spark awoke in the ashes, then another, then a third. They sizzled and darted back and forth among the dark lumps of coal till soon everything was consumed in a bright crackling flame. If Blümchen had been sitting in front of the oven door she would have seen all the same figures who one after the other had earlier frozen in place, but now they were stirring and wandering about the suddenly bright garden just as before but more lively and active. The handsome young man, too, was once again lying on the fiery red rose petals in the bower, reading his book, then closing it and kissing the red-hot cover. He then arose, left the bower, and motioned for his servants. He issued them orders and they scattered in every direction. The very next moment all of the rabbis and lords and ladies were standing in a circle around him, bowing reverentially. He said to them, "Be ready! For today I shall usher your queen into my palace and you shall enjoy a celebration like no other!"

Thus he spoke and, wrapped in a glowing cloak, he strode out of the oven. A hundred servants followed him. They bustled about the room with their censers, filling it with dense clouds and swathing Blümchen's bed with the sweetest fragrances.

The handsome young man, however, stepped closer to the bed and lifted the gently rustling bed curtains. There with heartfelt pleasure he beheld Blümchen as she slept: her brows arching over her closed eyes like two beautiful streaks of coal, and a peaceful smile playing on her lips like quiet glowing sparks twinkling back and forth. He leaned down and kissed her on her lovely mouth, saying: "You shall be my bride!" He then wrapped her in his cloak and bore her away.

When Blümchen awoke she was lying on an ottoman of the finest fire-red damask and wearing a thin robe that flowed down in the most graceful folds. Her dark tresses wound down her white shoulders like sportive serpents. When she looked up she saw she was in a strange apartment into which the loveliest red light fell through a large window of pure rubies, and everything—mirror and cushions, floor and walls, tables and flower vases—was bathed in a scintillating red shimmer.

She scarcely dared to breathe in all that splendor when twenty of the loveliest maidens appeared bearing precious veils and sumptuous garments and glittering jewelry. Before Blümchen could even ask where she was, who they were, and what they wanted, they knelt to the ground, crossed their arms across their chests, and kissed the carpets on the floor before her. One of them said, "We are you handmaidens, my Lady! Permit us to dress you!"

They then put the garments on Blümchen, wrapped her in the veils, and bedecked her with the glittering jewelry. They nestled a crown of rubies in her tresses, which they anointed with fragrant oils. And over her shoulders they lay a fiery red cloak, just like the one she had once embroidered for the queen. They then kissed the hem of her cloak and said, "Be ever kind to us, oh our Lady!" With that they left the apartment.

Our little girl let all of this happen, and for a long time after the handmaidens had disappeared she stood in the middle of the apartment staring in amazement at her reflection in the hundred mirrors and precious stones all around the walls. She no longer recognized herself; and she certainly would not have believed that it was she who was wearing the royal raiment had she not felt her own heart beating under the precious jewelry, and had she not distinctly heard that familiar voice calling: "Blümchen, my Blümchen, where are you?"

This time, however, it was not the voice of her mother returning home late in the evening, but rather that of the handsome young man pulling aside the flowing red curtain at the chamber's entrance and approaching her. He lovingly raised his devoted eyes to her beauty, bowed, bent a knee, and kissed her rosy fingertips. He then arose and said, "Follow me, fair queen! The grandees of the Empire have been waiting for an hour already!"

And as lovely and mute as a painting fresh from the painter's hand she walked next to him through the tall salons and halls and down the wide glowing marble staircase into the vast courtyard where the grandees of the Empire, all the lords and ladies, were assembled in their glittering outfits. Pages came forward with costly gifts, and just as Blümchen appeared choirs lifted their voices in thunderous music. All bent their knee before her, crossed their arms across their chests, and sang in unison: "Our greetings, oh lady, elect of thousands!"

At that, two immense folding doors opened, and she walked on the arm of the handsome young man into a magnificent temple, and the people and the grandees of the Empire and the pages and the musicians all followed.

In the rear of the temple, which was illuminated by the same soft rose-colored light as the rest of the palace, a small golden gate opened from within, beyond which a deep dusky chamber was visible. In the middle of the room rose a plain altar of white marble. Upon the altar a little star was glimmering, as if someone had just brought it down from the distant heaven and laid it there.

The handsome young man knelt at the threshold of the dark room, drawing our Blümchen down next to him. It was there she seemed to hear, calling from out of the darkling chamber: *Blümchen, my Blümchen, where are you?* She trembled in her heart and resisted the handsome young man. It was as if one hand were holding her back while the other was pulling her down, and she didn't know which to obey. But the one pulling her down was stronger and she knelt next to the young man.

Undulating tones rose as if from the distance, and a deeper, graver song filled the airy space of the temple, growing closer and closer. As the music swelled, stronger and stronger, the little star too began to expand in the dark room, becoming larger and more lustrous. The star seemed to move ever closer, as if from the distant heaven down to earth till it had become a great dazzling star, a white sea of light in whose shimmering splendor all eyes were blinded. Every heart and every pillar in the wide space quaked at the thunderous flood from the omnipotent choir, and no eye dared look up into the white sea of light.

A priest emerged from the dark room in the midst of which the brilliant star hovered over the altar like an immense ball of light. He spoke to Blümchen: "You renounce the faith of the earth and the delusion of man's heart and abandon the error of mortals in order to worship the all-blessing star!"

At this he dipped a golden chalice into the shimmering sea of light, raised it aloft, and displayed it to the assembled crowd, who all fell down in worshipful prostration. He then poured it out over the dark tresses of our Blümchen.

It drove through Blümchen's soul like fire and like molten coals through her every vein. She wanted to speak; she wanted to escape. But it was as if her tongue were bound and she were held fast with iron clamps to the step on which she knelt. She felt that some spell was controlling her, and that only one person was capable of unbinding that spell, and that that person was the handsome young man. He again kissed her fingertips and then her mouth, and the spell was broken, for she could now raise herself on his arm.

She walked back between the glowing pillars of the temple in which the assembled crowd cheered: "Hail the Queen!"

Four men were waiting at the temple's entrance carrying a fiery red canopy on four golden poles. The handsome young man and his young queen walked underneath it, and to song and jubilation they returned to the palace where everything had been readied for the most magnificent celebration.

At the head of a table so immeasurably long that both ends could not be seen at the same time Blümchen sat next to the handsome young man on a splendid throne. The guests sat on either side. A thousand servants scurried back and forth, serving molten embers in goblets of glowing gemstones and fragrant dishes in bowls of gleaming crystal. Everyone feasted in noisy delight and uproarious gaiety. The goblets clinked together, scattering sparks like fragments of shattered stars, their contents spilling like lava. And constantly echoing through all this jubilation came the cry: "Hail the Queen!"

So it went the whole night.

When morning again approached the handsome young man arose from his throne and led Blümchen out of the hall. He threw his cloak about her, leading her hastily behind the silk curtains of her bed and laying her there among her soft white cushions. Once again, he beheld her with the most blissful pleasure and kissed her lovely mouth. Then he said, "Farewell, my beloved bride! Soon you shall be mine forever!" and disappeared.

The bright embers in the stove died out as gradually as they had ignited, and when the widow awoke to prepare breakfast there was no spark left, only cold gray ashes on the bars of the grate.

The widow tiptoed softly around the room. She didn't want to awaken Blümchen from such a sweet morning's sleep. Was it not more dear to her than ever?

But when breakfast was already set at the table and Blümchen had still not woken up, the widow grew anxious, not knowing why her little daughter was sleeping so uncommonly late.

"I must have a look," she said. She walked over to Blümchen's bed and peeked through a narrow gap in the bed curtains at her beloved child who lay in a smiling slumber, so lovely yet so pale, so peaceful yet so completely different than usual.

"The child must have slept very little last night," she said to herself, closing the bed curtains tightly behind her and sitting down alone to breakfast. "I slept similarly," she went on. "I felt as if some ill would befall my Blümchen at any moment. I distinctly remember calling out to her several times in my sleep!"

It was nearly midday and the good mother had eavesdropped at the silk curtains innumerable times to catch the sounds of stirring behind it when Blümchen finally awoke, looking about in astonishment, not knowing whether to trust her eyes. She looked for the handsome young man, the lovely apartment, the radiant ball of light. And when she saw nothing but her white pillows and the green silk curtains and heard nothing but the voice of her mother asking *Blümchen, are you finally awake?* she got up dolefully from her bed and scarcely answered any of her mother's hundred questions. She remained quiet and mournful all day, and when her mother wished to leave again in the evening she began to cry and implored her, "Stay home, dear mother! I'm so afraid without you!"

So the widow stayed home for she thought our Blümchen was not well and sat next to her the whole evening in the warm nook by the stove. She told her many lovely stories till bedtime then blessed her little daughter and lay down to bed.

Blümchen, however, was beset by an inexpressible fear at the thought of going to sleep. She lay in bed but did not put out the lamp. Rather she set it on the little nightstand behind her bed curtains and read Psalms all night long until the bright morning streamed in. But since her mother hadn't noticed, she got up as early as usual and sang cheerful songs; she skipped about the house and helped the widow bake cakes. Tomorrow Rabbi Feivel, the goldsmith, and his son were to come, and the widow was glad that her Blümchen was well again.

But when she was alone, Blümchen sighed deeply, unable to stop the tears from coming to her eyes, for she was thinking about the handsome young man. Before nighttime she again grew frightened. As much as she desired to see him once more, she did not wish to sleep and stayed up praying all night long.

The Sabbath arrived and Rabbi Feivel and his son were a long time coming.

Jacob, Rabbi Feivel's son, was actually one of the most handsome young men in the city at that time. He was wealthy, and he was taken with lovely Blümchen. When the widow asked Blümchen whether she too liked Jacob she got no reply other than a flood of hot tears. But then her aunt and cousins came and talked to her, and before the Sabbath was over and candles could be lit, the engagement was concluded. An elderly aunt broke a lovely earthenware mug into little shards as a token that just as the mug could never again be made whole so the union should never be broken. One of the relatives, a young boy, ran in search of a scribe to write the betrothal contract.

The scribe arrived and the widow spread a white tablecloth over the table and lit two wax tapers. Everyone present sat down, and on a sheet of white parchment the scribe wrote out the contract that Blümchen and Jacob would be faithful to one another and love one another till death.

When all this had been written down everyone rejoiced, and the widow served a beautifully prepared dinner. But Blümchen did not wish to celebrate, returning Jacob's tender sympathy for her sadness with imploring looks, as if to say *Leave me, leave me be! I cannot be your wife after all, even if I did promise to; and should I become your wife, I could not remain so!*

Thus the evening proceeded amid the cheerfulness of the guests and the tears of the bride. It was arranged that the wedding would be celebrated in four weeks' time.

The guests had long bidden their farewells and the widow was still sitting at the table with Blümchen, speaking affectionately with her, making jokes about what would happen as she knew from personal experience.

It was an hour before midnight when they went to bed: the widow with the sweetest worries a mother can have, and lovely Blümchen with inexpressible fears. Amid the hundred ideas about how the wedding would be arranged the widow soon fell asleep, but Blümchen read her psalter. Weary from so much crying, exhausted from secret fears and the anxiety of two sleepless nights, she struggled in vain against sleep. He eyes finally closed against her will and she was heedless of the bell in the old cathedral tower toning twelve times, announcing midnight.

In the oven, however, everything came again to life.

Among the glowing walls of his palace and the flaming trees of his garden the handsome young man raged in a violent fury. He mustered his trusted followers who were racing this way and that, brandishing shining weapons and flaming torches. "Avenge me! Avenge me!" he cried. "The child of darkness whom I elevated to a princess of light has become disloyal to you and yet again you are bereft of a queen! Now you may once again wander through all the hearths of the world for a thousand years till you again become whole and till you may hope for liberation from the shackles of this mighty human race that has overpowered you and that you must serve to your ruination!"

They hurled looks seething with rage out into the twilit silence of the house lit only by the weak half-light of the little lamp which Blümchen had forgotten to put out as she fell asleep. In a moment the bright flames leapt up the silk bed curtains, and a minute later the whole house was aflame. The fire knocked out the window and swept up onto the roof. The alarm-bell atop the cathedral tower proclaimed: *Fire! Fire!*

The widow awoke, startled at the unusual heat in the house and at the uncommon brightness. "Blümchen, my Blümchen, where are you!?" were the first words she managed to get out as her heart filled with terror. "Lord God of Israel, just save my child!" she cried out in despair and thrust her long arms through the driving flames searching for her child's bed. Aglow and smoking the crossbeam in the ceiling collapsed, barring the way to her child just as God's flaming swords barred the way of the first man to paradise. But for an angel of God bearing her forth from the flames or being preserved in the fire as God's mercy once sheltered the youths in the fiery furnace her Blümchen was lost to this life. For lonely burned the little house on the riverbank, bereft of help, no call for rescue to be heard in the still night from the groaning of the cathedral's alarm-bell.

Wailing the widow rushed out into the night. "Maybe," she thought, "I shall find my child outside!" For the last thing to lose hope is a mother's heart and a mother's eye has the keenest vision through fear.

"Blümchen, my Blümchen, where are you!?" Plaintively she ran along the riverbank. But alas, all her plaints were for naught, as only the wails of the alarm-bell answered her cries of terror. This poorest of women had to watch with her own eyes as her house became prey to the flames, the falling rafters burying her only child.

Meantime morning had broken. The day laborers who had arrived to cut the ice found the widow keening and wandering despondently among the denuded walls of her house; they watched as she dug with her bare hands through the hot ashes and glowing coals of the still smoking scene of the fire. They heard her calling out, "Blümchen, my Blümchen, where are you?"

As rumor spread of the night's disaster, people started showing up, including Rabbi Feivel, the goldsmith, and Jacob, his son. No one knew how such a dreadful thing could have happened. No one had wanted to hear the alarm-bell, as if an evil spell had been cast over its agonized cries, prevented from finding their way into the heart of the sleeping city.

The poor widow, however, sat upon a charred beam, seeing no one, listening to no one, responding to nary a question. Only her tears sank into the ashes and her mouth called out from time to time: "Blümchen, my Blümchen, where are you?"

She lived for many years after that terrible night. She no longer embroidered in silk and velvet, and she stopped setting aside the lovely silver thalers. Rather, she managed to live off charity and slept at night in the community building, where the poorest and the homeless live. During the day she sat upon a charred beam at the scene of her house's fire, and rooted around among the rocks, speaking as if in a dream: "Blümchen, my Blümchen, where are you?"

After a days-long flood caused by an unusually strong ice drift a number of years ago, the charred site on the riverbank disappeared. Now the Moldau flows over it, and only periodically on windless days when the waves flow calm and clear is it glimpsed darkly from the depth of the current.

NOTES

(by the author, unless stated otherwise)

1 As is well known, the Jews lived at the foot of the Vyšehrad and in the Újezd before they were allocated the part of the city they later inhabited. They kept their prosperous warehouses below the Vyšehrad, which the chronicler Kosmas mentions repeatedly.

2 Chazan [*Chason*]: prayer leader.

3 Siddur [*sidur*]: prayer book.

4 Minchah [*Minchagebet*] is the afternoon prayer service and Ma'ariv [*Maariwgebet*] the evening prayer service.

5 Mezuzah [*Mesusa*], that is, doorpost. It is the duty of every Jew to attach a case made of glass, metal, or some other material and containing specific verses of the Holy Scriptures to the doorpost of his dwelling, so that he and his family and every stranger, when entering and exiting, may think of God, the refuge and light of Israel.

6 Lecha Dodi: "*Lecha Dodi likras kaloh!*" (Come, Friend, to greet the bride!) The first words of the hymn that introduces the Sabbath prayers.

7 Great Sabbath is the last Sabbath before Passover.

8 Mitsrayim [*Mizraim*]: Egypt, which is still referred to as *Mir* in the Middle East.

9 Haggadah [*Gadah*]: the name of the book which, in addition to a brief sketch of the suffering of Israel in Egypt, contains the prayers and songs prescribed for the first two night of Passover, along with various stories and allegories relating to the holiday.

10 "Bread of Affliction" is what the Haggadah calls the unleavened cakes that Jews eat in place of all other bread during the eight days of Passover. "Bitter herbs" are distributed to participants on the first two nights of Passover when certain passages from the Haggadah are read, as a symbol and reminder of the misery endured by their ancestors in Egypt.

11 According to Jewish law, consecration by the hand of the rabbi or a third party is not required for the marriage to be

concluded. It is sufficient for a man to give the girl he likes something of value, and for her to accept it, while reciting the words given in the story. The girl is then irrevocably his wife, and she is equally forbidden from becoming another man's wife as he is from leaving her and marrying another.

12 Sabbath Nachamu, the "Sabbath of Consolation," refers to the Sabbath following the Ninth of Av (the holiday mourning the destruction of the Temple in Jerusalem). Its name derives from the first words of a Biblical passage recited on that day. It begins *"Nachamu, nachamu 'ami"* ("Comfort ye, comfort ye my people" [Isaiah 40:1]).

13 Elul [*Ellul*]: the month before Rosh ha-Shanah, Yom Kippur, and Sukkot, a time dedicated to repentance and returning to God.

14 Ma'avar Yabok [*Maabir Jabok*]: "Crossing the River Jabbok"; a book containing Jewish prayers for mourning and burial.

15 Ninth of Av: the holiday mourning the destruction of the Temple in Jerusalem.

16 Old New Synagogue (*Altneuschul* or *Staronová Synagoga*): a storied Gothic synagogue in Prague's Jewish quarter, and one of the oldest active synagogues in Europe, completed at the end of te 13th century. (Translator's note)

17 Orach (pl. orchim): literally, "guest"; poor people (Author's note). Especially designates poor people who would be invited into people's homes for the Sabbath. (Translator's note)

18 Acher: Latin, *alienus*, one who is estranged, a stranger (Author's note). Especially a Jewish heretic. (Translator's note)

19 Bachur: young man.

20 Beit din [*beth din*]: a Rabbinical court. (Translator's note)

21 Chuppah [*chuppe*]: wedding canopy.

22 Sanhedrin: an assembly of elders who sat as judges in courts or tribunals in the cities of ancient Israel; the Great Sanhedrin was a kind of Rabbinical supreme court in the Second Temple period and into the 5th century. (Translator's note)

A collection of stories from nineteenth-century Jewish Prague calls for a few words about their author, Siegfried Kapper. Who was he? And what was his literary context?

Siegfried Kapper was born into a Prague Jewish family in 1821. Besides stints in Austria and South Slavic countries, he spent most of his life in Bohemia; he died in Pisa, Italy, in 1879, while being treated for tuberculosis. His first language was German, but his early education was to some extent bilingual in Czech and German. He received his university education first in Prague and then in Vienna, where he graduated as a doctor of medicine in 1847. In his early literary career Kapper distinguished himself as a mediator of Czech literature to German readership, which he did mainly by way of translation. He assembled an anthology of Slavic folklore (*Slawische Melodien*) in 1844, translated the major Czech romantic poet Karel Hynek Mácha into German, and continued this line of engagement well beyond the 1840s when he expanded his interest to South Slavic literatures. He also published in Prague periodicals of the time, above all two German-language venues, the journal *Ost und West* and the almanac *Libussa*, both important bases for German and Jewish Bohemian authors of the period. In the 1850s Kapper translated the so-called *Manuscripts of Queen's Court and Green Mountain* from Czech into German. While they were later discovered to be literary fakes, at the time he was translating them they enjoyed the aura of authenticity and were a monument of Czech national pride.

With this alone, Kapper would stand out as an engaged mediator between Czech/Slavic and German cultures, a function that gradually became part of Jewish intellectual identity in Bohemia. In the late nineteenth and early twentieth century, bilingual Bohemian Jewish authors and journalists cultivated this kind of engagement. However, although an early advocate of this path, Kapper distinctly transcended this approach with something that was unusual in his days—despite his first language being German, he published his earliest poetry collection in Czech: *Czech Leaves* (1846). This choice of language was a programmatic call to Bohemian Jews to join the emerging Czech national program and pay attention to its language. Reform Judaism and its positive attitude to diaspora may have played a role in this. A few Jewish contemporaries of Kapper's in the 1840s (Jacob Kaufmann, Leopold Kompert) were moving in a similar direction but, unlike Kapper, they continued to do so in German, thus continuing and asserting the German orientation of Jewish culture in Bohemia. Kapper's gesture incited a broad discussion. While heavily criticized by the prominent Czech critic Karel Havlíček Borovský (1811–1856), who simply rejected Kapper, claiming that a Jew cannot be a Czech poet, other Czech critics valued Kapper highly—his book was even nominated for a Czech literary prize.

Kapper was an advocate of Czech and Slavic cultures, but he was certainly not aiming at giving up his Jewishness by writing poetry in Czech. As he put it in his *Czech Leaves,* his program was not to assume Czech identity but live "in a union with the Czechs." In other words, his collection represents a discourse of fraternization—Czechs and Jews would share their homeland, Bohemia, and cultivate their shared bonds. Czech and Jewish authors close to Kapper (David Kuh, Václav B. Nebeský) tried to spell out this position in programmatic journalism, and, interestingly, some of Kapper's allies followed the rapprochement program by translating the Jewish prayer book into Czech, thus signaling to Bohemian Jews that they were local and that the use of Czech was appropriate even in religious life. However, all this was not as simple as it may seem even for Siegfried Kapper. Firstly, he continued to write mainly in German, and secondly, as the present collection shows, the stories he wrote indicate that Czech-Jewish symbiosis may lead to tragedies—at least in the past.

The three stories that appear here—"Genenda," "The Strange Guest," and "Glowing Coals"—were originally written in the 1840s. This was an era when literature in Central Europe was strongly marked by two genres—local tales and melodramatic stories about transgressive Gentile-Jewish romances. Both genres provide a background to Kapper's stories.

"Genenda," subtitled "From the Olden Days of the Ghetto of Prague," appeared originally in 1845 in the Prague almanac *Libussa*. Kapper presents the story as a genuine narration offered by an old Jewish man to his niece. Geneda's story is thus a story within a story—it is framed by the voice of a presumably authentic Jewish narrator. The authenticity of the story and its presence in Jewish memory is strengthened by the date of the action—Kapper places it as far back as the year 4000 of the Jewish calendar, a date he translates in a footnote as 1040 of the Christian era. The occasion for the narration is a romantic moonlit passage in a boat that leads past Vyšehrad, a cliff above the Moldau and the ancient seat of Bohemian rulers, at the foot of which an ancient Jewish settlement was still remembered. The story revolves around a romance between Genenda, the daughter of the local rabbi, and an aristocrat who, after falling in love with her, curries favor with the rabbi by pretending he is Jewish. The rabbi eventually agrees on Genenda's marriage with the stranger, but the entire story crashes the moment the groom reveals his identity by arriving at Genenda's home as a Gentile aristocrat with his "hundred knights" to take Genenda to his palace. It now turns out that she will obviously be wedded to a Gentile. Genenda is devastated: "Never! I can never be yours. You are alien to my race so you must be alien to my heart!" A series of gloomy episodes follows, peaking with Genenda's fall into the Moldau. It appears that she is trying to snatch her wedding ring that fell into the river—but in fact she commits suicide.

"The Strange Guest," in the German original "Der seltsame Orach," is also a work of the 1840s. It first appeared in the Prague periodical *Bohemia* in 1848. Unlike "Genenda," the story is fully embedded in Jewish ambiance in that it revolves around the classical *lieu de mémoire* of Jewish Prague, the Old Jewish Cemetery. In fact, the original title was "An Open Grave" ("Ein offenes Grab"). The Old Jewish Cemetery was a "mother of legends," where a tour from grave to grave amounted to a tour from legend to legend, yet Kapper seems to present his own invention—an earlier version or a later renarration of this story is not known. The compositional pattern resembles that of "Genenda" in that the actual story is framed, and hence authenticated, as a narrative offered by an old man who guards the cemetery. The story features a devoted Jewish man who wishes to transcend—and replace—Moses by uncovering the secrets that Lord communicated to him, but which were being kept hidden. He descends to an open grave to use it as a gate for a journey into the underworld during which he wants to accumulate arguments for his radical position. However, he returns after decades, showing no progress. He descends into the grave for a second time—to be now buried there. Specialists in fairy tales may find motifs here that were common in Czech and other fairy tales such as that of a youngster leaving his village in order to gain experience and return as mature man. But unlike this type of fairy tale, the strange *orach* returns home with a somewhat sober recognition that Moses could not be "reformed."

"Glowing Coals" first appeared in 1849, also in *Libussa*. And again, it is a doubly layered piece in which the narrator is a Jewish woman, the "old Malke." A family group is fittingly gathered around her at the fireplace, and while Malke says that one should not look into the fire too much as it excites imagination, she eventually recounts a story from the old days of the ghetto, where a widow is taking care of her daughter Blümchen, literally Little Flower. As the custom dictates, she finds her an appropriate Jewish groom and a wedding is in the making. Yet Blümchen is a victim of dreams. Gazing into the glowing coals in the fireplace before she falls asleep, she is possessed by reveries about a prince who takes her with him to his fairy tale kingdom. In other words, although Kapper does not say the prince is a Gentile, she is dreaming about a wedding out of the fold. The narrator locates the prince in a supernatural royal palace and describes him as the Prince of Light. In the meantime, however, the "earthly" process continues and the widow and the groom's father conclude a wedding contract. This enrages the prince, who wanted to raise Blümchen from darkness and elevate her to the Princess of Light. His underlings set the little house on fire, and as it burns down, Blümchen disappears with it. What remains is a forlorn site on the riverbanks marked by a few coals that seem to never extinguish. We can read the ending in two ways—on one reading, even dreams about crossing the dividing line between the worlds of Gentiles and Jews are bound to result in tragedy; or since Kapper does not say explicitly that the prince is a Gentile, on another reading we can conclude that marriage arranged against the will of those concerned is doomed.

The turn to tales was quite in line with a literature rooted in national histories and, in particular, local legends. A bibliographic survey of this period reveals dozens and dozens of Bohemian and Czech legends from the first half of the century, whereby legends are understood liberally as sagas, tales, even fairy tales. Paging through Hormayr's *Taschenbuch für die vaterländische Geschichte*, the influential Vienna-based periodical, a reviewer states with great satisfaction that "the results of research into internal and external history are often worked out as charming entertainment pieces for the reader." But while he thought that the "charming" world of tales and legends cannot be ignored by historians, literary authors did not hesitate to abandon historiography, however liberal, and engage with pure imagination. Kapper certainly did.

All the three narratives published here are Kapper's own creations. This needs to be noted as Prague Jewish legends typically revolve around documented historic personalities, Rabbi Ben Becalel Löw and his Golem being the best-known example. These stories have typically several versions and continued to be renarrated and even remediated for decades to come. However, the creative status of Kapper's tales should not deprive them of authenticity. Kapper was deeply influenced by Jewish life of his and his parents' generation as is sufficiently clear from a brief reflection from 1854, the year when he published a play titled *Ahasverus*. He noted on this occasion that Jewish oral folklore, including Purim plays, belonged to his deepest childhood impressions and added the recollection of a travelling fiddler, Itizig Fidele, who was wandering around and whom children made tell one story or another: "strange adventures in which kings and poor little Jews met each other in the forest, first walked arm in arm for a distance, then under a tree feasted together on roast goose and drank brandy, and finally recognized each other either as sons or fathers or one gave another his daughter's hand in marriage." This description is remarkable as it indicates that Jewish oral folklore did not exist in isolation and often approximated the world of Gentile romantic fairy tales of the period. The details of Kapper's note in fact point to stories such as that about how the poor Prague Jewish man Meisel became rich, which another author of legends, Leopold Weisel, published in *Sippurim,* a collection of popular Jewish stories published in Prague in the 1840s and 1850s.

Kapper returned to his tales in the 1850s with his novel *Falk*, in which he renarrated "The Strange Guest" and "Glowing Coals," adding two more pieces. It is characteristic that he again kept the model of a framed narration—they are all presented by Falk, the home preceptor, to the group of children he is bringing up. But it was not just a literary or historical interest that drove Kapper and other Jewish authors (Kompert, Weisel) to this narrative genre. Just as legends, again, broadly understood, were a prominent tool that cultivated the memory of diverse ethnic societies, they also asserted Jewish memory. A society that had legends—and cared for collecting, publishing, and even inventing them—could boast of a history of its own and qualify as a group worthy of respect. A gloss by a certain Julius Löwy, published in 1866 in the Czech literary magazine *Lumír*, echoes this. Publishing the Jewish Golem legend in Czech, Löwy boldly proclaimed: "Nowhere in the world do Jews have such beautiful legends as they do in Czech." Thus Bohemian Jews as a group deserved particular respect.

Kapper did not only benefit from the passion for tales that was lively in his days. His "Genenda" and "Glowing Coals" also echo literature that interrogated Gentile-Jewish relations, at least as they appeared in melodramatic narratives about transgressive romances of mostly Gentile men and Jewish women. This was another wave that was distinctly present in literature and theater of the first part of the century. This genre offered space for the reader to toy with the idea of transgression, yet most of these melodramatic stories end tragically, showing that romantic liaisons across religious lines violate the traditional order—quite typically in the tales, the Jewish women who cross the line die. "Genenda" and "Glimmering Coals" exemplify this. Genenda commits suicide when facing marriage with a

Gentile aristocrat, while Blümchen ends up in flames for her transgressive dreams. This is perhaps surprising. After all, Kapper was an advocate of a Czech-Jewish symbiosis: he wanted Bohemian Jews to live "in a union with the Czechs." We can only speculate what drove him to plots that in fact asserted the conservative order of things by punishing transgressions. Was it just the popularity of a literary genre that drove these plots or did he want to say that crossing the line belonged to the tragedies of the past?

Jindřich Toman
University of Michigan

ABOUT THE TRANSLATOR

Jordan Finkin is rare book and manuscript librarian at the Klau Library of Hebrew Union College in Cincinnati. A scholar of modern Yiddish literature, he is also a literary translator from Yiddish, German, and French. Dr. Finkin is the founder and director of Naydus Press, a non-profit publisher of Yiddish literature in English translation.

CONTENTS

MODERN CZECH CLASSICS

Published titles
Zdeněk Jirotka: *Saturnin* (2003, 2005, 2009, 2013; pb 2016)
Vladislav Vančura: *Summer of Caprice* (2006; pb 2016)
Karel Poláček: *We Were a Handful* (2007; pb 2016)
Bohumil Hrabal: *Pirouettes on a Postage Stamp* (2008)
Karel Michal: *Everyday Spooks* (2008)
Eduard Bass: *The Chattertooth Eleven* (2009)
Jaroslav Hašek: *Behind the Lines: Bugulma and Other Stories* (2012; pb 2016)
Bohumil Hrabal: *Rambling On* (2014; pb 2016)
Ladislav Fuks: *Of Mice and Mooshaber* (2014)
Josef Jedlička: *Midway upon the Journey of Our Life* (2016)
Jaroslav Durych: *God's Rainbow* (2016)
Ladislav Fuks: *The Cremator* (2016)
Bohuslav Reynek: *The Well at Morning* (2017)
Viktor Dyk: *The Pied Piper* (2017)
Jiří R. Pick: *Society for the Prevention of Cruelty to Animals* (2018)
Views from the Inside: Czech Underground Literature and Culture (1948–1989), ed. M. Machovec (2018)
Ladislav Grosman: *The Shop on Main Street* (2019)
Bohumil Hrabal: *Why I Write? The Early Prose from 1945 to 1952* (2019)
*Jiří Pelán: *Bohumil Hrabal: A Full-length Portrait* (2019)
*Martin Machovec: *Writing Underground* (2019)
Ludvík Vaculík: *A Czech Dreambook* (2019)
Jaroslav Kvapil: *Rusalka* (2020)
Jiří Weil: *Lamentation for 77,297 Victims* (2021)
Vladislav Vančura: *Ploughshares into Swords* (2021)
Jan Zábrana: *The Lesser Histories* (2022)

Forthcoming
Jan Procházka: *Ear*
Ivan M. Jirous: *End of the World. Poetry and Prose*
Jan Čep: *Common Rue*
Jiří Weil: *Moscow – Border*
Libuše Moníková: *Verklärte Nacht*

*Scholarship

MODERN SLOVAK CLASSICS

Published titles
Ján Johanides: *But Crime Does Punish*

Forthcoming
Ján Rozner: *Sedem dní do pohrebu*
Gejza Vámoš: *Atómy Boha*